Cooly .A.

THE WINTER WAR

THE WINTER WAR

A NOVEL

WILLIAM DURBIN

WENDY
LAMB
BOOKS

Published by Wendy Lamb Books
an imprint of Random House Children's Books
a division of Random House, Inc.
New York

Wendy Lamb Books and colophon are trademarks of Random House, Inc.

Visit us on the Web! www.randomhouse.com/kids

Educators and librarians, for a variety of teaching tools, visit us at
www.randomhouse.com/teachers

Library of Congress Cataloging-in-Publication Data
Durbin, William.
The Winter War / William Durbin. —1st ed.
p. cm.
Summary: Although no other country will come to Finland's aid when Russia invades the independent nation during the winter of 1939–40, Marko, a young polio victim serving as a messenger boy in the Finnish Army, and the soldiers in his squadron are determined to keep their homeland free.
Includes bibliographical references (pp. 228–29).
ISBN 978-0-385-74652-6 (trade)—ISBN 978-0-385-90889-4 (lib. bdg.) 1. Russo-Finnish War, 1939–1940—Juvenile fiction. [1. Russo-Finnish War, 1939–1940—Fiction. 2. Soldiers—Fiction. 3. Poliomyelitis—Fiction. 4. People with disabilities—Fiction. 5. Finland—History—1939–1945—Fiction.] I. Title.
PZ7.D9323Wg 2008
[Fic]—dc22
2007007048

Printed in the United States of America

10 9 8 7 6 5 4

First Edition

*To the brave citizens of Finland who defended
their homeland during the Winter War*

❧

*And to my grandson, Linden Reid Durbin, in the
hope that wars will one day be no more*

FOREWORD

Imagine the leader of a powerful nation deciding to invade a smaller country and liberate its people. He orders his army to attack, assuming that this country, whose people have recently experienced a civil war and great hardships, will welcome his soldiers with open arms and strew flowers at their feet. The leader plans on a weeklong war.

Though this situation might suggest more recent events, the war, which became known as the Winter War, began in the fall of 1939. Earlier that year Joseph Stalin, the dictator of Russia, had threatened to take land from eastern Finland for "security reasons." President Kyösti Kallio of Finland tried to negotiate a compromise, but Stalin refused.

2   The Finns turned to Field Marshal Gustaf Mannerheim for help in building up their defenses. They mobi-
lized their army and set up observation posts along the
border to study Russian troop movements, hoping the
whole time that war could be avoided. . . .

November 30, 1939

Virtalinna, Finland

CHAPTER 1

THE WATCHTOWER

Marko scanned the dark eastern sky with his field glasses.

"What time is it?" Johan asked.

"Five minutes later than the last time you asked."

The cold scent of pine needles drifted through the open window of the Virtalinna church tower.

"School will be starting soon." Johan pulled out his pocket watch and struck a match on his boot to see in the winter darkness.

"Can't you ever follow rules?" Marko blew out the flame. "You know the army put a blackout in place."

Johan snapped his watch shut. "Twenty minutes to nine."

"I thought I heard something." Marko brushed his

white-blond hair out of his eyes and focused the glasses on the horizon, searching for a glint of silver that might be a Russian plane. Marko and his best friend, Johan, were junior members of the Civil Guard, and they'd been taking their turn as sky watchers in the eight-sided bell tower of the old church since August.

"If you stare hard enough, you can imagine anything," Johan said. "Did I tell you the one about the banker and the priest?"

"Forget your jokes!" Marko kept his glasses fixed on the sky. A faint pink light glowed above the distant hills. The forest below the church tower was quiet, but the town behind Marko was coming to life. A whistle blew over at the ironworks, and a train chugged into the station across the river as a horse pulling a coal wagon clopped down the frozen street in front of the church. Marko could hear the people making their way toward their stalls in the marketplace.

"We'll be late for school," Johan said.

"The next sky watcher should be here any minute." Marko set down his field glasses and grinned when he saw the snowflakes on the windowsill. "Any more snow, and you'll have to leave your bike at home."

"I'm riding my bike until Christmas." Johan stood up and slipped on his black leather gloves. As the son of the superintendent of the ironworks, Johan was the only boy in Class VI who could afford a bike. Marko's father owned a small blacksmith and knife-forging shop, so Marko's only hope of getting a bike was to build one out of used parts.

"You'll give up that bike when you face the first snowdrifts."

"I don't care if it snows every single day." Johan grinned. "It didn't stop me on Independence Day."

Marko laughed, his blue eyes brightening. Last year on December 6, Finnish Independence Day, Johan had tied a Finnish flag on the handlebars of his bike and lit a railroad flare on his rear fender. Then he pedaled through the snow as people waved and laughed.

"My bike ride was more exciting than the mayor's speech."

"Your father didn't think so," Marko said.

Johan grinned. "His scolding was nothing compared to the sparks from that flare burning the seat of my pants."

"I don't know how your father can be serious all the time when your mother is so jolly," Marko said. "I'll bet she already has her Christmas party planned."

"She's ordered twelve dozen—"

"Wait! What was that?" Marko said.

Pretending to listen, Johan turned his head and made a little birdcall by whistling through his teeth.

"Stop it!" Marko raised his hand. "I really do hear something."

A deep humming vibrated in the cold air like the lowest note on a giant pipe organ. The boys had been trained to listen for the engines of a Russian DB-3 bomber. Now that they'd finally heard a plane, they could only stare at each other.

Marko grabbed the field telephone, cranked the handle, and picked up the receiver. The line to the Civil

8 Guard headquarters was dead. He cranked it again. Still no sound.

"We've got to warn headquarters!" Marko shouted, but Johan beat him to the stairs. Marko cursed his left leg—weakened by polio three years ago—as he scrambled down the narrow stairway.

By the time Marko rushed outside, Johan had pedaled halfway down the block. The sound of the bombers was loud and close.

Marko ran; his weak ankle swung outward, and the metal brace on his leg clacked each time his heavy boot hit the street. "Watch the corner," Marko yelled.

Marko hit an ice patch and fell. When he jumped to his feet, a mother and her little girl stepped out their door with a market basket in hand.

Marko yelled, "Take cover," as he scrambled to catch up with Johan, but the mother only waved and smiled. "Bombers!" he yelled as he ran. "Go back."

The cobblestoned streets of Virtalinna were so narrow and crooked that when Marko reached the first corner, Johan was already out of sight. At that same moment Marko saw a blur of silver in the sky to his left. Three bombers approached, blunt noses angled down. One plane banked left and one right, while the middle bomber bore straight toward Marko.

People had stepped outside their small wooden houses to check out the noise. "Bombers!" Marko shouted. "It's a raid."

Those close enough to hear ducked back inside, but others peered into the sky. Marko felt as though he was caught in a bad dream as he watched the far plane dive lower. When the first bomb was released, it glided forward, racing the plane. Then it arced downward, followed by a trail of more bombs. Where was the alarm? Why hadn't Johan reached headquarters yet?

The growl of the middle plane turned to a roar. The ground trembled as Marko tilted back his head and saw a red star on the underside of the wings.

Then Marko heard a whistling sound. "Cover!" he yelled, diving into the nearest yard.

Before Marko hit the snow he saw a bright flash. The sound of the bomb blast slammed into his body. The ground trembled, and it felt as if a great wave was lifting the street.

He covered his head as rubble rained down. The ground shook as more bombs hit in the distance.

His ears rang as he stood up, dizzy and sick. Blood ran down the fingers of his right hand. The snow was black with soot, and thick dust hung in the air. Just ahead, a smoke cloud hung over a twenty-foot-wide crater. The explosion had sucked the glass out of every window in sight, and a large linden tree was split down the middle. The house beside the crater was gone except for the stone chimney; splintered furniture, broken crockery, and shredded curtains and bedding were strewn across the sidewalk. A headless porcelain doll lay in the snow.

Marko's heart raced as he ran past the smoking wreckage of the house, his feet crunching on broken glass and bits of wood and mortar. Though the roof and walls had been blown away, the breakfast fire still smoldered behind the stone hearth, and snowflakes fell with tiny hisses into the coals.

A man yelled, "Someone get the doctor!"

Marko watched the whole world crumble around him. Houses tilted in odd directions. Telephone wires drooped to the ground. A brick wall was riddled with pieces of shrapnel, and wooden shingles littered the street. Flames rippled from the roof of a house beside a second crater.

Long after the last bomb had exploded, the air raid siren finally blared. Marko jogged into the city center and turned onto the main avenue. Smoke floated above the bare birches in the park.

When Marko reached the market, vendors were climbing out from behind their stands and staring at the ruined street. Vegetables, straw, baskets of eggs, milk cans, bolts of cloth, and weaving materials were scattered everywhere. A horse thrashed in its traces beside an overturned wagon, whinnying like a hurt child. Coal had spilled onto the street, and the driver was struggling to unbuckle the horse's harness.

Then he saw the bomb crater beyond the wagon. A bicycle lay beside the jagged hole, but Johan was nowhere to be seen. Marko rushed forward praying, *Let Johan be safe.*

When Marko saw the black gloves he skidded to a stop and put his hands on his knees to steady himself. His heart pounded as he gulped in the cold air and tasted spent powder in the back of his throat. The gloves, locked to the handlebars, held the bloody stumps of Johan's hands.

CHAPTER 2

AMID THE RUINS

Marko stared at the gloves and the crater.

"Have you heard anything about the school?"

"What about the children?"

Marko turned. A woman faced a guardsman.

"They hit this side of town," he said. "The children should be safe."

Children! His little sister, Nina, had walked to school alone that morning!

Marko took off running. Nina must be terrified.

By the time Marko reached the school, a dozen parents were ahead of him. He pushed through to Nina's classroom, where she dashed forward and hugged him. "Marko? Are the Russians coming to kill us?"

"Don't talk like that, Nina," her teacher said. Turning

to Marko, the teacher added, "Your sister has been very brave. So have all the children."

"I'm proud of you." Marko took Nina's hand. "We'll get you right home. The planes are gone now."

Marko and Nina rushed up the winding street that led to their farmhouse. Marko peered ahead as they rounded the last corner. Ah! Their front gate stood straight and true. A fresh dusting of snow lay on the roof, and the "Koski's Forge" sign that Marko had helped Father paint hung over the double doors of their barn.

Mother ran outside with Marko's little brother, Jari, in her arms. "Marko! Nina!" She set Jari down and dropped to one knee to hug Nina. "I was about to run to the school—" Mother stood up when she saw the tears in Marko's eyes. "Are you hurt?" She touched his shoulders and looked him up and down.

"No." Marko wiped his eyes with his coat sleeve.

"Thank heavens."

"It's Johan," Marko said.

"Oh no! What happened?"

"He was on his bike." Marko closed his eyes and took a breath. "A bomb—"

"Oh, Marko. Not Johan. No, no, no . . ." Everyone was crying, and Mother tried to hold all of her children in her arms.

As he wept, Marko felt cold and alone. *This can't be happening. It can't.* Yet there was no denying the picture locked in his head of a black crater and blood-spattered stones.

Marko spent the rest of the day helping the Civil Guard pick through the rubble and search for survivors. But he avoided going near the street by the Guard headquarters.

Despite the dozens of bomb craters and collapsed buildings in town, only four people had been killed.

Every time Marko lifted a splintered timber or a broken stone, he kept thinking how Johan had always been lucky, so lucky. It was impossible that he could be gone.

Marko was exhausted that night, but he couldn't sleep. Every time he closed his eyes he saw the bicycle and the black gloves.

As he tried to doze off, he recalled the day he'd come home from the hospital after four months of polio treatments. A cast covered his leg from the knee down.

As soon as Mother helped Marko into bed, she told Father to bring a saw in from his shop. When he returned, she said, "Either you cut it off or I will."

"But the doctor—" Father began.

"Doctors don't know everything," Mother said.

Marko said, "I promised to keep the cast on for six more weeks."

"I've nursed enough people to know what happens when a person doesn't use his muscles." Mother worked as a midwife, helping the local doctor with his childbirth cases. She was also a member of the Lotta Svärd, a volunteer corps of women who helped the soldiers. "This cast is coming off, and if your father isn't willing to help, I'll do it myself."

Mother reached for the saw, but Father pulled it back. "I don't like the idea one bit," he said, "but I'll not have you butchering his leg."

"Cut along here." Mother drew an imaginary line down the cast. "But don't go all the way through." She picked up a scissors from the dresser. "I'll snip the wrapping with these."

Marko stared at the sharp teeth of the saw. "The doctor said I'd be crippled if I tried to walk too soon."

"Didn't the same doctor say you caught your polio from touching rotted maple leaves?" Mother said.

"My teachers warned us about those leaves, too."

"And they were wrong." Mother waved her scissors. "You didn't get sick from playing with leaves. And you won't get well by lying flat on your back." She turned to Father. "Would you move that saw!"

Father started sawing, and the dry, dusty smell of plaster filled the bedroom. Marko closed his eyes. Mother believed hard work could fix everything. What if her stubbornness undid the healing of his long hospital stay?

Marko squealed when the saw teeth nicked his ankle.

Then a siren wailed.

CHAPTER 3

SHELTER FROM THE STORM

As Marko's memory faded, he saw black sky outside his bedroom window. *Sirens!* He sat bolt upright. *An air raid! Get to the shelter.*

"Are you awake?" Mother stood in the doorway.

"I'll bring Jari." Marko climbed out of bed.

"Nina's already up," Mother said.

Squinting in the dim light, Marko sat on the cold wooden floor and slipped on his leg brace. He laced up the half shoe that was connected by two metal slats to a leather collar below his knee. Then he pulled on his pants and boots. He picked up four-year-old Jari, asleep beside him. Jari never woke as Marko cradled him in his arms and hurried to the kitchen.

Nina cried, "Don't make me go into that smelly hole."

16   "No time for tears." Mother pulled Nina's hand. Mother's favorite expression was "Speak your mind or be silent." At five-one, she was two inches shorter than Marko, but her perfect posture—she urged all her children to "stand tall"—allowed her to look him straight in the eye.

Outside, the Bofors antiaircraft guns started firing from near the ironworks. Jari clamped his arms around Marko's neck.

The sky was cold and clear, and the snow on the woodshed roof sparkled in the starlight. The siren kept wailing as Marko led the way past the barn.

The Koskis' log farmhouse was the last building on the south side of Virtalinna. It stood beside an open field overlooking the deep blue waters of Lake Keskijarvi. The moonlight in the birches reminded Marko of the many times he and Johan had hiked and skied through the forest that surrounded the lake. Just last month they'd won second place in an orienteering contest. Though Marko couldn't run fast, he had the endurance to ski all day long, and he was good at reading a map and compass.

Marko opened the outer door of the root cellar and climbed down the steps ahead of Mother. The low room had been dug into the hillside for storing vegetables. At harvest time Marko helped Mother fill the wooden bins of the root cellar with potatoes, onions, turnips, and rutabagas. Carrots were buried in clean sand. The dirt floor gave the room a musty smell.

"The scent of earth reminds me of planting time,"

Mother said. "I get so lonesome for my garden in the winter."

"It's cold down here. And stinky," Nina said.

Marko set Jari on a bench and closed the doors. His plump-cheeked brother yawned and rubbed his eyes. Then Marko knelt and lit the homemade lantern he'd fashioned out of a coffee can and a candle. "Isn't that better?"

Nina hung on Mother's arm. "I'm freezing." She shivered like a little bird. Marko wrapped a blanket around Nina's shoulders, and Mother held her close.

The antiaircraft fire was now mixed with the drone of bomber engines.

"The lantern makes it nice and cheery," Mother said. She ran her free hand through her shoulder-length blond hair. Then she straightened Nina's golden braids.

"I wish Papa was home," Nina sniffled.

"Marko's here to look out for us." Mother patted Marko's arm. "And he's getting to be almost as strong as your father."

Marko laughed. "I'll believe that when I can swing a four-pound hammer like he does." Marko recalled how Father's arms rippled with muscles when he pounded on his anvil.

"I want Papa," Nina said.

"We all miss Father," Mother said. "But we must be brave."

Father, a veteran of the 1918 civil war, had been called up for duty last month. Two soldiers had knocked on the bedroom window at midnight, waking up the whole house. They handed Father a stamped document, ordering him to report to the train station. While Father dressed in his Civil Guard uniform, Mother packed some rye bread and cheese in his rucksack, and Marko helped brush his boots and clean his rifle. Then Father hugged Mother and the smaller children, shook Marko's hand, and strode off into the darkness.

Now Marko looked at the jars of water and the blankets that he'd set on the shelf last month, just in case they needed the shelter. "I didn't think Russia would ever attack us."

"We were all hoping for the best," Mother said.

"Russia promised us our independence back in 1917 when they got rid of their czar!"

"The history books might say that. But Russia never liked the idea of a free Finland. It was only a matter of time before they made up an excuse to start a war."

The ground shook as a string of bombs exploded nearby. "What about Tuuli?" Nina jumped off Mother's lap.

Tuuli was their gentle workhorse, and Nina adored her. The family's second horse, Teppo, had been "drafted" into the army.

"Tuuli's safe in the barn," Marko said as the earth continued to shake.

Jari explored the room. Grinning, he waved at his own shadow on the wall.

"We need to put out the candle," Marko said.

"Don't make it dark!" Nina said.

"You know the blackout rules." He bent down and blew out the flame.

Jari climbed onto Mother's lap and bounced on her knee. "Sit still," Mother said. "Would you like a song?"

"A funny one, Momma," Jari said.

Marko smiled. Mother sang beautifully in church, but at home she liked to make up silly words to old folk tunes.

"How about 'My Pretty Darling'?"

"Yes!" Jari clapped his hands.

" 'My darling is so very pretty,' " Mother began in a singsong rhythm. " 'With her skinny bones and her knotted hair, with her squinty eyes and her yard-wide mouth, she makes the horses in the market laugh.' "

Jari and Nina giggled and joined in for the second verse.

While they sang, Marko stared into the darkness and tried not to close his eyes. If he did he would see the jagged crater and the gloves all over again.

Suddenly a bomb hit so close to the cellar that Nina screamed. Dust sifted between the roof planks and down the back of Marko's shirt.

"Poor Tuuli." Nina's voice trembled.

"Everything will be all right," Marko whispered.

But Marko wondered: Would anything ever be right again? How could he have fooled himself into believing a war wasn't coming? The Russian farmers who traded in Virtalinna were honest, hardworking people, but he should have known better than to trust the Russian government. Father often told Marko stories of what it had been like during his boyhood, when Russia controlled Finland. The czar angered everyone by making Russian the official language of Finland. Then he banned the

Finnish parliament and began drafting Finnish men into his army. The bitterness toward Russia peaked during the Finnish civil war, when Russia contributed to the bloodshed by supporting Red forces within Finland.

"More," Jari said, urging Mother to sing another song.

As Marko thought back over the last few months, he could see so many signs that war was approaching. Early in the fall the Finnish government had announced a rationing program for coffee and sugar. That same week Marko's class started making gas masks in school. A blackout policy required people to paint their lampshades black except for a little point of light. Workers dug a deep, zigzag trench in the park and covered it with logs and earth to make a bomb shelter. Schools were even closed for a time during the mobilization of troops.

But the oddest thing of all had happened toward the end of summer when Marko and Johan were walking past the church. A well-dressed couple stopped them. "What sort of a factory might that be?" The man spoke with a strange accent as he pointed to the furniture company across the river. Then he asked about the ironworks and the sawmill. Marko and Johan answered politely, and the man gave them five marks each.

The boys ran home, anxious to tell Johan's father about their good fortune, but Mr. Kronholm said, "Those people may have been Russian spies. You must be careful whom you speak with these days."

At the time Marko had thought Mr. Kronholm was worrying too much. Now Marko knew—he'd helped two spies that day.

The explosions were further apart and fainter now.
Nina was beginning to breathe easier.

Marko hadn't been the only one who believed war could be avoided. Even Father remained positive on the night he shouldered his rifle and prepared to catch the troop train. "Building up our defenses is only a precaution," he told Marko. "Field Marshal Mannerheim is too wise to be drawn into a fight. He's pulled our men well back from the front so there's no chance a stray bullet can start something. I'll be back at my forge by Christmas. But in the meantime"—he glanced at Mother and the smaller children—"can I count on you to look after things?"

"Of course."

Father's first letter from the front said he'd been assigned to a post in the north. He couldn't tell the family where, but he gave a hint in his final sentence: "We won't have to worry about an attack unless the Russians trade their tanks for reindeer."

But no matter how far north Father might be, Marko knew he couldn't escape the Russian bombers.

They stayed in the shelter until the church bell rang after sunrise. "All clear." Marko stood up.

"Don't leave us, Marko," Nina said.

"I need to see if it's safe." Marko walked to the door and listened. He heard the faint clanging of a fire bell.

"No, Marko!" Nina cried. "The Russians will get us."

"The planes are gone." Mother squeezed Nina's hand.

Jari made the sound of a bomber and laughed as Marko climbed the steps and opened the second door. Their farmhouse and barn were all right. He called down: "Everything is fine. Tuuli's safe."

Marko looked to the east. The sky above the lake was milky gray. When he turned toward town, he saw smoke from dozens of fires merging into an angry black column. The fire bell clanged and shouts echoed from the city center.

The smell reminded Marko of the midsummer bonfire that had blazed beside the river last June. The townspeople sang and danced all night. As the flames died down toward morning everyone was sleepy and ready to walk home, but Johan challenged the boys to a fire-jumping contest. "Marko, you judge who leaps the farthest," he said, not wanting his friend to be left out.

When Johan tried to jump the widest part of the fire on his first effort, his foot brushed the embers and his shoelace caught on fire. But he lined right up to try again. Soon everyone was laughing and cheering.

Today, through the smoky haze Marko could see the flagpole above Kronholm Castle. The twin flags of Sweden and Finland hung limp against the white pole. Marko imagined Mrs. Kronholm wringing her hands and pacing back and forth in her drawing room, grieving for Johan.

CHAPTER 4

THE FUNERAL SLED

On the morning of Johan's funeral, Marko walked to the barn before dawn to feed and water Tuuli. When he got back to the house, Mother was setting a pan of water on the cookstove.

"I'll make rye porridge. We need a hot meal before church," she said. Birch bark and kindling crackled in the firebox, and a thin puff of smoke rose from under the stove lid.

"Do we have to put out the fires during the day again?" Nina asked.

"That's the new blackout rule," Mother said. "No cooking after sunrise." Mother's blue eyes, which were normally bright, looked gray and tired today. She often teased Marko, saying, "You inherited my eyes but your father's head," meaning that Marko was blue-eyed like her but stubborn like Father. Though Father never wavered from a task, Marko had never met anyone more stubborn than his mother.

"But it gets so cold." Nina hung on Mother's arm.

"We can't let the Russian pilots see the smoke," Marko said. "We'll just put on three coats if we have to."

Nina gave him a little smile.

Jari was so sleepy that he laid his head on the kitchen table. Marko looked out the window into the starless black sky. Snow was gently falling. "The clouds should keep the bombers grounded."

"That will help us bury Johan in peace," Mother said. "I never thought I would dread clear skies."

Marko sat down and rubbed his calf.

"Sore?" Mother asked.

"A little."

As he rubbed his leg, Marko thought back to the August afternoon three years ago when he'd first felt the pain. He and Johan had been swimming. They'd been going to the lake all summer long, and they were both tanned and strong. But on the way home Marko got so tired that he could barely walk. Then his left leg began to ache. He tried not to limp, but Johan asked, "What's wrong?"

"It must be a cramp."

"Lucky that didn't happen when we were swimming to the island," Johan said.

"I would have sunk like a rock." Marko tried to smile.

That evening Marko felt good enough to eat a big dinner. But he got dizzy later and threw up. Father said, "I told you your eyes were bigger than your stomach."

Marko was so tired that it took all of his strength to walk to his bedroom and crawl into bed.

The following morning he woke with a high fever. Father brought the doctor home after church. The doctor said Marko had a case of the grippe, an illness like the flu, and he left some medicine. But Marko ached a hundred times worse than he ever had from the flu. And he couldn't stop sweating. Mother held a cool cloth against his forehead, but he burned with fever all night long. His left leg felt as if it was being jabbed with needles, and he couldn't help groaning. At times he arched his back, and his whole body went rigid from the pain.

The next morning he felt better. But when he tried to get out of bed, his leg crumpled under him, and he fell. The minute Marko saw Mother's eyes he knew something was very wrong.

"Momma?" Nina's voice pulled Marko back to the present.

"Yes, dear?"

Mother had pinned her own hair up, and now she was getting Nina ready for church. "How can they have a funeral for Johan if they can't find all the pieces of his body?"

"Whoever told you such a thing?" Mother set her comb on the table and looked at Nina. Marko's stomach churned as the image of the smoking crater and the bicycle flashed back.

Nina said, "I heard Mrs. Arvilla talking to her husband."

"You know she likes to gossip," Mother said. "Johan was a good boy. He's safe in God's arms."

The Koskis walked to church under a leaden sky. For Marko the fresh snow normally would have meant getting out the sleds for the children, hitching up the sleigh for the first time, and waxing his skis. But today the snow held no joy other than the relief it offered from the Russian bombings.

All of Johan's classmates and teachers came to the funeral. When Marko opened the church door for Mother, he heard a whispered *"Rautakinttu."* Iron Leg. He turned but saw only grown-ups. Iron Leg was the hated name that some boys in school called him because of his brace.

On Marko's first day back at school after his recovery, the teasing had hurt almost as much as his polio had. He'd worked so hard to push himself to walk again, but a group of boys pointed at his brace and laughed. No one else in his school had caught polio, and he wanted to tell his classmates the whole story. How he'd lain flat on his back in the hospital for two weeks. How he'd struggled for two months before he was strong enough to hold himself up between two chair backs. How he'd taken his first steps with crutches. And finally, how proud he'd been to walk for the first time in his new brace.

Over time Marko had learned to use the teasing to make himself stronger. He blocked out the words in the same way he fought the pains that shot up his leg with a burning, electric jolt. He worked harder than everyone else. To make up for his weak leg he built up his arms and shoulders so no one could beat him at arm wrestling. And if anyone told him he couldn't do something because of his leg, he fought to prove them wrong.

Johan had been one of the few boys who never teased him. Last spring when he and Marko were fishing below the mill house, Marko asked, "So why didn't you ever make fun of me?"

"Why would I?"

"You know." Marko rapped the metal slats under his pant leg as he watched his cork bobber float in the foaming current.

"I'd never tease a friend. And they pick on me, too."

"Your father owns half this town."

"It's hard when everyone thinks you've got it so easy." Johan cast out his line. "They call me 'poor little rich boy,' you know. And how would you like it if your parents lectured you every single day? 'Do the Kronholm name proud.' "

"I thought you liked being descended from royalty."

"I'd give anything to be just plain Esko or Eero or Eino."

"You're kidding."

"No." Johan jigged his bobber.

Marko was shocked. The Kronholms had three servants, while he and Father worked six days a week to make ends meet. Father was a farmer, blacksmith, and knife maker. Together he and Marko shoed horses, tended a crop of rye and potatoes, and repaired everything from plowshares to gate latches at their forge.

"We should trade places someday just for the fun of it," Johan said.

"Just for the fun of it."

But they never did.

Today, as Marko took a seat in the old timber church and bowed his head, he knew that not one person in Virtalinna would dream of trading places with the Kronholms.

The local Civil Guard commander conducted Johan's funeral with full military honors. Six guardsmen pulled the pine coffin on a sled to the front of the church and carried it inside.

Other than Mr. Kronholm and a handful of men who were too old for military service, the church was filled with women and children. As the organ played, Marko heard a note that sounded lower than normal. He looked at the organ loft and listened hard. Had the sky cleared for another attack? Everyone looked toward the door, waiting for the air raid siren.

The Guard commander stood up. "No need to worry. It's one of our Fokkers."

A collective sigh went up as everyone eased back into the pews. If only the Finnish fighter planes had been on patrol the morning of the first attack!

As the minister led the prayers and hymns, Marko followed in a daze. The worst part was the stiff praise of the eulogy: "Johan was a fine young man, a servant to God's will . . ." Marko didn't want words; he wanted his best friend back. Whom would he talk with at school now that Johan was gone? Whom would he hike and fish with?

Later, when they lowered Johan's coffin into the grave, tears welled up in Marko's eyes. Mother squeezed his hand. During the minister's final words, snow began to fall again. Three more dirt piles covered with green canvas stood nearby; those people had also died in the bombing.

Marko shuddered as the first clod of earth hit the coffin lid. Johan's mother sobbed; she was shaking so badly that Mr. Kronholm had to steady her.

As Marko and his family walked through the cemetery gate, Marko heard two guardsmen talking.

"You know how this war started! The Russkies fired artillery on their own troops and blamed it on Finland!"

"Stalin's a black heart." The other man was grim. "He wanted this war, even if it meant murdering some of his own."

Stalin was the Russian dictator. Marko knew he was evil—yes, he had a black heart. But how could any man shell his own soldiers?

And how could Finland defeat such an enemy?

CHAPTER 5

THE ROAD TO SAVOLAHTI

Marko slapped the newspaper down on the breakfast table. "Isn't Sweden going to help us? They're supposed to be our ally! Do they expect us to fight the whole Red Army on our own? I can't believe that England or America won't help us."

"No one has the courage to step forward," Mother said. "Now that Stalin has taken Estonia and Latvia, every country is afraid they'll be next. And America is making so much money selling arms to Russia. Who knows if they'll help?"

A knock came at the front door, and Mother jumped up to open it. She turned white when a boy handed her a telegram. Marko stood beside her: *Don't let it be bad news about Father*. Mother held her breath as she opened the envelope. "Papa's fine—it's not about him. But things are bad at Grandma's."

"Are the Russians close?"

"They're evacuating the whole area."

Momma's mother lived in Savolahti, a small village forty kilometers east of Virtalinna. She'd been a widow since 1918, when Red forces killed her husband during the civil war. Her farmhouse was only ten kilometers from the Russian border.

"Should I get the wagon ready?" Marko asked.

"Yes, and I'll see if Mrs. Arvilla will watch the children." She set off for the neighbors'.

Nina followed Marko to the barn. "Can't I ride to Grandma's with you?"

"The wagon would be too crowded," Marko said, but he was thinking about the danger near the front.

Marko opened the barn door and looked at the cold forge and the leather apron hanging on the wall. The empty blacksmith shop made him lonesome for Father. When Marko was little, Father let Marko put one hand on the handle of his hammer and pretend he was helping pound out a horseshoe or a knife blade. Marko loved watching the sparks fly and listening to the clink of the hammer on the anvil. Knife making was the most fun because whenever Father plunged a red-hot blade into the tempering tank, he'd wink and say, "Now we cool the steel in our bucket of dragon's blood—that makes the strongest blades!"

But before Father let Marko near the forge he'd taught him the "blacksmith's boot dance," showing him how to jump back quickly if a bit of white-hot steel landed on his clothes. "You don't want to look like this," he said, holding out a forearm that was peppered with small scars from metal burns.

Nina's voice brought Marko back to the present. "Good morning, Tuuli," she said, reaching into the stall. The pretty chestnut mare whinnied and perked up her ears, and Nina stroked her neck. Though Tuuli was sixteen years old, she was a hard worker. Like all Finnish horses, she was broad in the neck and shoulders, and she could pull 110 percent of her weight.

Beyond the stall Marko saw a pile of used bicycle parts. Father had promised to help him build a bike this winter, but none of that mattered now. He stared at a rusty fender and thought of Johan racing along on his bike.

"Can I help you hitch up Tuuli?" Nina asked.

"Good idea!"

While Nina got the bridle, Marko looked at Teppo's empty stall. He missed their young gelding. Last October, as Finland prepared for the possibility of war, the Koskis had been ordered to deliver Teppo to the army. When Marko brought Teppo to the railroad depot, the district horse officer snipped a two-number code and their family name into Teppo's coat, so the horse could be returned after the war.

"Will you take good care of him?" Marko had asked.

"A horseman looks out for his mount before he tends to himself," the officer had said.

Now they finished hitching Tuuli to the wagon as Mother walked back with their next-door neighbor, Mrs. Arvilla.

Mother knelt and hugged Nina. "Nina, please keep an eye on Jari." Mother kissed both children on the cheek.

"I won't let go of him." Nina held Jari's hand as Mother climbed onto the wagon seat beside Marko.

"They'll be fine, Marja," Mrs. Arvilla said.

Mother waved as Marko clicked his tongue to start the horse.

The Savolahti road was the only route out of Virtalinna to the east. It followed a high ridge between thirty-kilometer-long Lake Keskijarvi and the swampland to the north.

"The army tore up the road moving their equipment to the front," Mother said.

Marko nodded as the wagon bumped along in the frozen ruts. Despite the blanket that covered their legs, the steel slats of his brace felt like ice.

When the wagon hit a hole and lurched toward the ditch, Marko's left leg slipped off the footrest. He tried not to wince.

The pain reminded Marko of the day Mother had taken off his cast and begun exercising his leg. It made no difference that he complained about the saw cut on his ankle. "We have to work hard," she said. "Muscles wither and die if they aren't used."

Five times each day she wrapped strips of hot, wet wool around his leg. Then she pulled his leg straight out and held his foot against the footboard of his bed. Just when Marko was ready to cry from the scalding heat and the pain of having his cramped muscles stretched, Mother took off the prickly wool. Then she flexed his knee and rotated his ankle. "Make it move," she said, tugging so hard on his leg that Father had to pin Marko's shoulders to the bed so he wouldn't slide off.

"Why not just put me on a torture rack?" Marko asked.

"One day you'll thank me," Mother said.

No matter how hard Mother worked, Marko's leg felt dead, like a piece of wood. His skin was pale from being under the cast, and his calf had shrunk to half its normal size. "The doctor said I might never walk again."

"He had no business saying such a thing," Mother said. "Feel your muscles move." She flexed his leg and pummeled his calf with the heels of her hands. "Believe, believe . . ."

Long after Marko had given up hope, Mother kept working on his leg. Through the spring she stretched and pulled and prodded his muscles. Between exercise sessions Marko lay in bed, looking out at the other children playing. Johan was the only one who ever visited. "Still taking it easy?" he'd tease before he gave Marko a book or a treat that his mother had sent along.

Then one day when Mother pulled on Marko's ankle, a muscle twitched deep down in his calf.

Mother beamed at him. "You felt something, didn't you?"

Marko's eyes filled with tears.

"Marko moved his leg!" Mother ran to the kitchen.

The whole family crowded into the bedroom to congratulate him. Father picked Jari up from the floor and held him level with Marko's eyes. "Look at your big brother! He'll be chasing you around this house before we know it."

The sight of a woman driving a hay wagon piled high with household goods brought Marko back to the present. The road was crowded with evacuees fleeing from the front. A boy and a dog trailed behind the wagon, along with a flock of sheep.

Further on, they met an old man on foot leading a milk cow. He carried a backpack with a hunting rifle strapped across the top. And a young mother held a baby tight to her chest as her two-wheeled cart bounced over the ruts. The same look of disbelief was frozen on everyone's face.

Late in the afternoon Marko pulled Tuuli up to rest on the hill overlooking the village of Savolahti. Mother looked on her childhood home and said, "I can't bear to think about what's going to happen."

The river beyond the small cluster of houses was glazed with new ice. The town held only three hundred people, but for two centuries Savolahti's famous pottery factory had been firing crocks and vases from the red clay of the valley.

"The fighting must be getting close." Marko eyed the smoke rising off the far ridge. The dull thud of artillery shells exploded in the distance.

"Let's hope Grandma's safe." Mother squeezed Marko's arm.

Partway down the narrow road that wound into the

village, Marko heard heavy equipment. Soldiers were working in the spruce forest, camouflaging machine gun emplacements. At the base of the hill the army engineer corps was finishing a line of tank traps, trenches, and barbed wire fences.

"I'll bet they're using some of the wire you and Johan collected," Mother said.

In the fall the Junior Civil Guard had collected war materials. Marko and Johan had driven a wagon from farm to farm asking for donations of clothing, blankets, boots, tools, harnesses, skis, lanterns, and barbed wire. Johan was a master at talking people into contributing. "Now that it's butchering time," he said to a farmer who had just sold his beef cattle, "you won't be needing that barbed wire fence."

Not only did the farmer donate the wire, but he also helped the boys pull the staples from the fence posts and coil the wire in the wagon.

"I've got scars to prove how good Johan was at convincing people." Marko held up his finger to show the white scar from a wire cut.

"You were lucky to have a nurse in the house that day to bandage you up," she laughed. Then she paused. "I know how much you miss Johan." She patted his leg.

The only sound Marko heard as he drove into the village was the creaking of the wagon springs. The empty streets felt eerie. For the first time in Marko's memory no smoke rose from the chimneys of the pottery factory. The shard pile was dusted with snow. As a little boy Marko had often picked up pieces of pottery imprinted with the fancy SP crest and skipped them across the river.

Marko stopped the wagon in front of Grandmother's house, where a skinny soldier stood with his cap in his hands, talking with Grandma. She wore a white apron and kerchief and held a broom in her hands. "Ma'am," the soldier said, speaking very slowly, "don't you know we have to burn your house down? No need to clean."

"I understand perfectly well," Grandma said. "But a gift to one's country should be delivered in the best possible condition."

The soldier walked away shaking his head.

"What was he talking about?" Marko asked Grandma. The house smelled of freshly baked bread.

"If the army can't defend the town," Grandma said, "they have to destroy everything that might aid the enemy."

Mother hugged Grandma. "Surely not our home!"

"You know we burned this house once before on account of the Russians in 1918. We can rebuild." Grandma's white kerchief framed her round face. Her blue eyes were clear and alert.

"But all our work!" Mother said.

"The soldiers know their business." Grandma squeezed Mother's hand.

"Hurry, we'll pack your things," Mother said.

"Those nice soldiers said we'll be safe until morning," Grandma said. "Let's sit down and have a cup of coffee. I just baked some *pulla*."

"Tuuli comes first," Marko said.

He drew a bucket of water from the well and blanketed and watered Tuuli. Just as Marko started back toward the house, the thin soldier appeared and knocked on the door again.

"Sorry to bother you again, ma'am." A stocky soldier beside him held up a rusty bicycle.

"Yes?" Grandma walked to the door.

"Is this your bike?"

The bike made the picture of the jagged bomb crater flash through Marko's mind.

"That old thing belongs to the neighbors," Grandma said, "and they've already left town."

"We're gonna use it for a booby trap." The thin man grinned.

"You expect a Russian to pick up that wreck?" Marko asked.

"It don't have to pedal. All it takes is one poor devil to test the seat. I'll rig a charge to give that Russkie the ride of his life."

"How perfectly horrible!" Mother said.

Marko shivered at the thought of an exploding bicycle seat.

"You'll have to excuse Kekko," the short man said. "We're the demolition team, and he gets real excited when he talks about blowing things up."

"I'm the demo man," Kekko said. "But some of the boys call me the undertaker."

"He's done some fine work over there." The short man pointed at the house two doors down. "He boobytrapped the outhouse seat, the cellar door, and the woodpile. But his best trick was the dead chicken."

"You wired a chicken to explode?" Marko was amazed.

Kekko laughed. "If a Russkie so much as tickles her tail feathers his goose will be cooked."

"We need to finish up the mayor's house," the short man said. "We got a grand party planned. After we torch the village, we figure the Russkies will pick that place for their headquarters. So we wedged a dynamite surprise up the chimney."

"As soon as she heats up—*Kablam!*" Kekko grinned as they walked off.

Marko stepped back into the house. Grandma's parlor looked clean enough to host a wedding. The floor was polished, the windows were washed, and the furniture was dusted.

"Could you please carry that to the wagon, Marko?" Grandma pointed at a trunk that Mother had packed with dishes and silverware. "If we get everything loaded tonight, the soldiers can do their job as soon as we leave in the morning."

"How can you be so calm?" Marko asked.

"A house is only a shell to keep the rain off our heads," Grandma said. "It would be selfish to complain. My grain sacks are full. My grandson is here to watch over me. Life hasn't always been so easy in this stump-ridden land. I can remember winters when we ground up birch bark for flour and fed our horses twigs. We Finns are tough because the weak ones starved or froze. Those Russians must not know that the men we have left are the toughest bulls in the pasture."

"You've given the soldiers a head start on their

work." Marko nodded at the neat pile of kindling and the kerosene can in front of the fireplace.

"To complete my gift to Finland," Grandma said.

The next morning Mother stood in the front yard and stared at the house. "If only there was some other way," she said. Across the river ragged flames rose from roofs of homes the soldiers were already burning.

Grandma took Mother's arm and they walked to the wagon.

By the time Marko had clicked Tuuli to life, Kekko and his friend were walking toward Grandma's house to do their work.

Grandma sat between Marko and Mother and never turned her head as they passed burning haystacks and soldiers shoveling manure down wells. The Finns weren't going to leave anything behind that could help the Russians. The road smelled of smoke and cold mud. Marko's eyes burned from the yellow smoke clouds. Tuuli sneezed as they passed a truck buried to its axles in the ditch. Grandma patted Marko on the arm. "It's good that you brought a strong horse."

The crackling of the burning houses and barns sounded like a forest fire behind them.

When they reached the top of the hill, Marko stopped the wagon to rest Tuuli. As the horse blew hard, Marko looked back on the village one last time. Smoke billowed up over the river and drifted east, where the Red Army marched under snow-crowned pines, drawing ever nearer to the town.

CHAPTER 6

THE TRAIN TO SWEDEN

"Grandmaaaa!" Nina ran up to the wagon with Jari trailing.

"Have you been staring out the window all day?" Mother asked.

"They've taken turns," Mrs. Arvilla said. "They couldn't wait to see their grandmother."

"Who are these grown-up children?" Grandma asked.

"Grandma!" Nina shouted. "It's me, Nina, and Jari."

"You can't be Nina Koski." Grandma shook her head as she climbed down from the wagon. "My Nina is only this tall." She held her hand level with Nina's ear.

"That was last summer. Stop teasing!" Nina said.

With a chuckle, Grandma knelt and hugged Nina and Jari.

* * *

December, a dark month in Virtalinna, turned even darker. Churches and schools were closed. Not only were house lights blacked out, but people also had to paint over the headlights of their cars, leaving only slits. Everyone draped their windows with dark cloth and hung blankets over the inside of their doors. The whole town seemed to be in mourning.

One night after supper, Mother set Nina on her lap and asked, "Would you be willing to do a good deed to help your country?"

"Like Marko serving in the Civil Guard?" Nina asked.

"Yes. It would mean a journey. As a Lotta, I'll be working long hours helping turn the school into a hospital, and we need to find a safe place for you and your brothers. Grandma and I were thinking of sending you to Sweden. Grandma would go along."

"Sweden!" Nina looked stunned. "Where our cousins live?"

"In Gothenburg." Mother paused to keep herself from crying.

"I've nothing to hold me here," Grandma said.

"Would you do that to help the soldiers?" Mother asked.

Marko expected Nina to wail, *Why me?* But she nodded. "If it will help the soldiers."

"I'm so proud of you." Mother bit her lip as she looked across the table at Grandma.

Nina asked, "Could we have a fire and a warm meal during the day in Sweden? I'm so tired of being cold."

"Of course, dear." Mother stroked her hair.

After Nina and Jari had gone to bed, Mother turned to Grandma. "Are you sure there isn't some other way?"

"The children aren't safe this close to the front. And with Marko's help, traveling with them should be no trouble."

"I don't want to run away to Sweden," Marko said.

"It isn't safe here," Mother said.

"What about you?" Marko said.

"My work in the Lotta Svärd is important to the war effort," Mother said. "And I have to be here when Father comes home."

"The Junior Civil Guard is important, too."

"But think of what happened to Johan. I need to know you're safe!"

"I need to help defend our homeland!"

The morning was dark and cold when Marko drove the family to the train station. To cheer up the children, Mother sat in the back of the wagon and made up a song about a princess named Nina and a young squire named Jari, who were traveling to their winter palace in a sleigh pulled by white horses.

"In a golden sleigh, away, away," she sang. Though Mother tried to smile, Marko could tell she was on the verge of tears.

When they arrived at the depot, a big Tampella

steam locomotive was already idling beside the platform. Black smoke puffed out of its tapered stack, and snowflakes swirled in the bright beams of its triple headlights.

Nina remained brave. "We're doing this for Finland," she told Jari, repeating Mother's words as she climbed out of the wagon with her little pasteboard box in her arms. Last night Mother had packed the box with Nina's best yellow dress—the one with small red and blue flowers—along with her carefully darned stockings and her doll. Mother had told Nina, "You must be a big girl and help Grandmother take care of Jari."

Unlike Nina and Jari, most of the children at the station were traveling alone. Sweden had agreed to take in child refugees so that Finnish women could work full-time, staffing first-aid stations and hospitals and doing volunteer work. One local woman had even signed on as an army sniper.

Marko watched a young mother kneel in front of her son to say goodbye. She straightened the name tag that hung around his neck. "You must never take this off—no matter what." Her eyes were filled with tears. "Promise me?" Her son's name was printed on the tag along with his family name and address. *Virtalinna* was written as the start of the journey, but the *goes to* line was blank.

Nina tried to read the boy's name tag. "What's that spell?"

"Ilmari." The boy wiped his tears with his sleeve.

"You can sit with us on the train," Nina said.

Grandmother smiled at the boy. "Ilmari is a fine

name. Not only can you sit with us, but if your mother doesn't mind, I may have a peppermint stick for you."

"How kind of you," the mother said.

"I'm sure that Ilmari will be a good traveling companion," Grandma said. "Let me introduce you to Jari."

Mother pulled Marko aside. "It's not too late for you to—"

"We've been over this a hundred times," Marko said. "I'm staying. To fight." He tried to turn away, but she held both his hands.

Mother rarely cried, but she was on the verge of sobbing. "I'd never forgive myself if—" She pulled out a handkerchief and dabbed her eyes. "I mustn't let the little ones see me like this." She took a shaky breath. "But I can't bear the thought of something happening to you. I couldn't go on. You'd be safe in Sweden. And—"

"And I couldn't live with myself if I didn't do my part here."

Mother closed her eyes and nodded. "Dear Marko . . . I've taught you too well."

As soon as everyone had boarded the train, the station manager waved his hand. The engineer gave two short blasts on his whistle and opened the throttle. The pistons sped up with a loud *huff, huff, huff,* and smoke shot from the stack. The drive wheels spun on the icy rails for a moment before they caught.

Only when the train jerked forward did the reality hit Marko: Grandma and the children were leaving! For the first time he realized that his family might never be together again.

Mother and Marko trotted beside the children's car the length of the platform, waving, while Nina and Jari pressed their faces against the window. Mother remained brave until the last car pulled away. Then she and the other women burst into tears. One young woman dropped to her knees in the snow and sobbed.

Marko hugged Mother. "I should be with them," she cried softly, "to look out for them."

Marko tasted the bitter acid of coal smoke in his mouth as he watched the light on the caboose fade into the darkness. There was no turning back now. Would he be of any use here on the home front? Or would folks laugh at him as the iron-legged boy who should have gone to Sweden with the babies?

CHAPTER 7

THE HOSPITAL

The next morning Marko volunteered to help Mother at the hospital and refugee center that had been set up in the Virtalinna school. As they walked from the edge of town, they both carried a white sheet so they could lie in the snow and cover themselves up in case of an air raid.

The only thing that looked different about the school was a Red Cross flag hanging above the door. But once they were inside, Marko saw that everything had changed. The main hall was piled with crates of medical supplies and linens. Carts were parked beside the class-room doors. Both nurses and Lottas in white-collared uniforms and caps hurried down the halls. Many of Mother's Lotta friends helped at the hospital, while others worked throughout the town as cooks, telephone operators, and aircraft spotters. Women had also filled the men's jobs at the ironworks and the sawmill.

Marko began his day in the gymnasium helping serve bread, coffee, and milk to the refugees. They were mainly women and children from villages near the border, who had no relatives to take them in.

As Marko handed a mother milk for her toddler, she asked, "Have you heard when the train will pick us up?"

Marko didn't know what she meant, but a Lotta said, "The new list will be up this afternoon, Sonja. We'll post it on the bulletin board by the door."

The Lotta turned to Marko. "Families from all over Finland are volunteering to house people. As places become available, these folks are sent out on the train."

Through the morning Marko shelved supplies, went to the post office, and mopped the floor in his old Class VI room. The beds in the room were empty because the train had just taken several wounded soldiers to a hospital in central Finland.

When Marko finished cleaning the floor, he looked out the window at Kronholm Castle. Through the gently falling snow he could see the blue cross of Finland and the gold cross of Sweden on the flags above the castle wall. This time of the year Mrs. Kronholm would normally be decorating her dining hall for her upcoming Christmas banquet. The vaulted hall, which used to be a chapel, had been Marko and Johan's favorite place to play when they were little. It had a twenty-foot-long table with two dozen high-backed chairs and a cande- labrum as tall as a small boy. Handwoven tapestries covered the walls, and a three-story-high leaded-glass window overlooked the river. At Christmas the window was hung with spruce garlands and bright ribbons. But this year Kronholm Castle was draped in black.

If only he could turn time back to the morning before the first bombs fell!

A voice called, "All personnel report to the lobby immediately."

When Marko got to the front entry, the head nurse said, "I am sorry to report that the Russians bombed the hospital train."

"But how could they? The cars have big red crosses painted on the roofs!" a nurse said.

"The first of the injured should arrive within the hour."

"That may be them right now." Mother pointed out the window at two sleighs heading toward them.

Marko met the first sleigh at the back door. The driver and the soldier were both dressed in whiteovers, camouflage against the snow. Their jackets and pants were crumpled and stained with soot and dirt. As Marko and the driver slid the stretcher under the soldier, he gritted his teeth. His face was ashen, his right thigh soaked with blood.

When they carried the wounded man through the back door without bumping him, he looked at the driver and grinned. "Finally a smooth ride. Arvo must have hit every rut between here and Savolahti."

"You were at Savolahti?" Marko said.

The soldier nodded and took a shaky breath. "We surprised the Russkies last night. Routed them. I was the only one hit."

"But we nearly got fitted for wooden overcoats on the way here," the driver said.

"Wooden overcoats?" Marko asked.

"Coffins."

Like Johan, wearing a wooden overcoat and sleeping in the cold, cold ground.

"A fighter plane attacked us," the driver explained.

"That nearly gave me a double coronary to go along with this shot-up leg," the soldier said.

"You can't have a double coronary when you've only got one heart," the nurse laughed.

"I say a Russian fighter with machine guns blazing can give anyone a double heart attack." Then the soldier whispered to Marko, "She's a cute one. You suppose you could line me up a date after the doc sews me back together?"

"I heard that," the nurse said.

"I was hoping you would."

Before they had the last of the wounded soldiers in bed, the first victims of the train attack began to arrive. Twenty-seven people had been injured and six killed. Two of the dead were good friends of Mother.

Marko was shocked as he helped carry in the wounded. One soldier had been cut so badly by shrapnel and glass that he reminded Marko of a rabbit run over by a hay mower. Another soldier who couldn't stop moaning had a bandage wrapped around his head and eye. An unconscious young Lotta had a thick bandage on her right hand. "A bad cut?" Marko asked the man helping him carry the stretcher.

"Her fingers are gone," he whispered.

The burns were harder for Marko to take than the blood and the mangled limbs. Every time he leaned over a body the smell of smoke and burnt flesh made him gag.

Most of the soldiers took their injuries without complaint. The bravest of all was a thin fellow whose stomach wound had been torn open during the attack. "I'm a no-good-luck soldier," he said, trying to smile. "Those Russkies have my number."

Marko helped all night as they struggled to stabilize the patients while repairs were made to the tracks.

When he and Mother walked home for a rest in the middle of the morning, Marko's leg was so sore that he had to swing his hip out to the side with each step. Wearing his brace so long had rubbed his leg raw.

Marko said, "I didn't think hospital work would be so tiring."

"Men always think women's work is easy," Mother said.

At home she rubbed Marko's leg with a salve that she'd made out of pine tar, lard, and honey. After a short nap they were back at the hospital.

When the rail line was opened in the afternoon, everyone helped take the wounded to the train station.

As the staff stood on the platform, waving goodbye, Marko noticed a man was missing. "Where's the soldier from Savolahti?" he asked.

"Not everyone made it," Mother said.

"He died?"

She nodded slowly.

Marko thought, *How many more good men will be joining Johan and the man from Savolahti before this war is over?*

It was well after dark before Marko and Mother started home. "I feel like I've skied to Grandma's and back," he said.

"The patients appreciated every step you took today," Mother said.

Marko looked up at the stars. "I hope this clear sky doesn't bring more air raids." The siren had gone off twice the night before, but the bombers had passed high overhead on their way to attack the interior of Finland.

"Maybe they think Virtalinna is bombed out," Mother said.

"Let's hope—" Marko stopped when he saw a man in a black coat riding a horse at the top of the hill. It was their minister. He was the one who brought families the news when soldiers had been killed. Marko and Mother didn't breathe until the minister turned onto a side street.

"Thank heavens it wasn't us," Mother whispered. She looked to the north. "Let's pray that Father is safe tonight."

CHAPTER 8

THE LIEUTENANT'S BREAKFAST

Two days later Marko stepped into the dusk to help carry in a wounded officer. As Marko approached the sleigh, the man slid off the back. His right arm was in a sling, and his whiteovers were stained with blood. "Let me help you, Lieutenant," the driver said.

"I wasn't shot in the leg." The lieutenant grabbed the side of the sleigh.

"Be careful, sir!"

"I'm not an invalid." The lieutenant stared at Marko. "That you, Koski?"

"Mr. Juhola!"

"For a minute I thought you'd forgotten your old teacher."

"No, sir," Marko said. Should he salute? Mr. Juhola had been his toughest teacher.

"So how's the leg?"

"Fine, sir," Marko said, embarrassed that his teacher would mention his leg.

"Here we are back at our old schoolhouse." The lieutenant started up the steps.

As Marko held the door open, Mother ran forward. "Why is no one helping this man?"

"My fault," Lieutenant Juhola said. "I ordered them not to." Now that they were inside, Marko noticed he was very pale.

"Well, we're in charge in this hospital," Mother said. She put the lieutenant's good arm around her shoulder and steered him into a room.

He smiled. "They're demoting me to Class I, Koski. I never was patient enough to work with the little ones."

His last words were slurred, and he suddenly slumped forward.

"Just as I thought." Mother tipped him onto the bed as he passed out.

Marko said, "He acted like there wasn't anything wrong."

"Officers are always the worst patients. They're very bad at following orders."

The sleigh driver nodded. "Soldiers get so hopped up in the rush of the battle, they can't even feel they've been hit. Once the adrenaline wears off, they collapse."

* * *

The next morning Mother said, "You can bring the lieutenant his breakfast."

"Can I wait on someone else?"

"You should be proud to help your teacher," Mother said.

"But—"

"It makes no difference that he wasn't your favorite."

As Marko picked up the bread and coffee in the kitchen, he thought back to how much he'd disliked Mr. Juhola's class. The only thing Juhola cared about was sports. Before he became a teacher he had qualified for the national track team, and he was a training partner for the Olympic champion Paavo Nurmi, the Flying Finn.

Sports were difficult for Marko in his brace. Skiing was the only sport he could do well, because he could glide forward. But they didn't teach skiing in school.

Mr. Juhola was an army reserve officer, and each morning he put the class through a series of exercises. He was fond of saying, "We must be prepared if the need ever comes to defend our homeland." During the afternoon recess he coached the class in the current sport.

In the fall Mr. Juhola focused on *pesäpallo*, Finnish baseball. He said the motion of throwing the ball was the same as tossing a hand grenade, and that base-running was like the rush of an attacking infantryman. He chose the two best players as captains to pick the teams, and Marko was always the last boy chosen.

*   *   *

"But the doctor has ordered bed rest." Marko heard a voice as he walked down the hall. Marko reached the lieutenant's room as a Lotta came out.

"Good luck with him." She rolled her eyes.

When Marko stepped into the room, the lieutenant was standing at the window and looking down on the bridge and Kronholm Castle. A gentle snow was falling outside.

"Good morning, sir," Marko said.

Juhola turned. "Morning, Koski. It feels odd to be in our old school. I get the urge to write the day's lessons on the chalkboard." He stood ramrod straight, and his piercing blue eyes were bright.

Marko handed him a plate with a slice of rye bread covered with jam.

"Lingonberry?"

Marko nodded. "Is your arm feeling better, sir?"

"Good as new. The doc set the bone—I told those medics at the front to snap it back in place and save me a sleigh ride, but they wouldn't do it. Doc sewed up the bullet holes, too."

"You were shot?"

"Just two small wounds in the shoulder. The doc did fine for a Swede." The lieutenant grinned. "Speaking of Swedes, how's your buddy Johan?"

"He was killed in the first bombing raid."

"No!" Juhola looked shocked. "I'm sorry to hear that. I liked Kronholm." He sat on the bed and sighed, shaking his head. "Not young Johan . . . I used to think the Russian pilots were killing civilians because their aim was so bad, but now I'm convinced they're following orders."

"Bombs have destroyed more than thirty homes," Marko said. "But at least they haven't knocked out the bridge."

"I don't believe they've tried to hit it." The lieutenant sat thinking. "Johan. I am so sorry." Finally he took a bite of bread.

Marko handed him a cup of coffee. "They could trap us on this side of the river if they blew out the bridge."

"They'd be trapping themselves, too."

"Why would—" Marko stopped and thought. "Unless they planned to cross the river right here."

"Everyone thinks the Red Army will keep hitting the southern front until they break through our defenses on the Mannerheim Line. But they've already thrown a crack regiment at us here. If they can drive through Virtalinna and into central Finland, they could cut our supply lines and use our railroads to move their troops behind our southern forces."

"Bypassing the Mannerheim Line altogether," Marko said.

"Exactly."

"Isn't a regiment two thousand men?" Marko asked.

"Two thousand seven hundred." Juhola sipped his coffee. "But our lone battalion has stopped them cold so far."

"A battalion is only five hundred men!"

"We have to hold this front at all costs. Luckily, we have a friend the Red Army hasn't factored in."

"Another country is sending troops?" Marko snapped to attention.

The lieutenant shook his head. "Sweden, Britain, and America are all afraid of Stalin. Right now we're standing alone." He walked to the window. Snow was falling from the gray sky. "No, the friend I'm talking about is right out there. Winter is a familiar companion to us, but for the city boys from Moscow and the poor recruits they ship in from the south it will mean white death."

CHAPTER 9
JUST THE WAY IT IS

The next morning Marko returned to Juhola's room with breakfast, anxious to ask him if he'd heard any news from the north, where Father was stationed. The patient was dressed and shaved. "You're not leaving already?"

"I've got to get back to my men. It's not right for me to be pampered by the nurses while my men are sleeping in tents."

Mother walked in behind Marko. "You should be in bed."

"There's a war going on," the lieutenant said.

"Your arm hasn't mended. There's a risk of bleeding or infection."

"As much as I appreciate your concern, I have no

choice. But I'm glad you're here. I've been meaning to talk with you."

"About what?" Mother asked.

"I could use Marko's help."

"Hasn't he been taking good care of you?"

"He's been doing a fine job, Mrs. Koski," Juhola said. "In fact, with your permission I'd like to sign him on as a messenger with my command group. We need someone who knows the area around Savolahti."

"Marko? He's too young!"

"Athletes make outstanding messengers."

"I'm no athlete," Marko said. "I was lousy at baseball and every other game you had us play."

"But I noticed how well you and Johan did in those weekend orienteering contests. You have a good sense of direction, you can read a compass, and you ski fast."

"You followed those events?"

"I did my share of orienteering when I was your age."

"What about Marko's leg?" Mother asked.

Marko said, "You told me to never use my leg as an excuse."

"Not the front lines!" Mother said. "I couldn't bear it."

"You've always said I can do anything I set my mind to."

"I'd keep him well back from the action, Mrs. Koski," the lieutenant said. "He'd be delivering messages for our company."

"But—"

"Mother! This would be my chance to serve Finland!" Marko said.

"Exactly," the lieutenant said. "The thing I admire most about Marko is that he never gives up. A struggle always brings out the best in him."

Marko was shocked. *Praise from Juhola?* He turned to Mother. "Father would be proud that I could do my part."

She looked at Juhola. "There's no way you could keep him safe out there."

"Life doesn't come with guarantees, Mrs. Koski, but I'd do my best. And there is no greater honor for a man than to serve his country."

"He's just a boy." Mother looked at Marko and her eyes welled up with tears.

"You've always taught me to believe in myself. If I can beat polio, I can deliver a few messages to the soldiers."

"You don't have anything more to prove!" Mother said.

"Mother—we're fighting for freedom, for honor!" Marko said. They looked at each other.

Finally Mother said, "I never dreamed . . . not my Marko." She turned to Juhola. She was crying now. "You'd promise to watch out for him?"

"I knew you wouldn't stand between a man and his duty to his country."

A man! Marko thought as Mother hugged him.

"I'll watch him as if he were my own son, Mrs. Koski." Then the lieutenant extended his hand. "Welcome to Company Three, Marko."

"Thank you, sir." Marko shook his hand.

"But from now on you can drop the *sir*. Working soldiers don't have time for formalities."

Me a working soldier? Marko thought as he walked to the doorway. When Marko had first joined the Junior Civil Guard, Father teased him about being a boy soldier—a member of a "squirrel company," he called it. But with a single handshake Marko had joined the company of men.

He stepped into the hallway, wondering: *Will I be up to the task?* And a deeper worry nagged him: *How can an army of farmers, blacksmiths, schoolteachers, and boys stop a trained force of 2,700 Russian soldiers?*

Two days later a knock came at the door in the middle of the morning. Mother looked out the window at the soldier who stood in front of the house. "Not already?" she said. "This is too much like the day we said goodbye to Father." She quickly wrapped up some bread and cheese and stuffed it into Marko's pack.

Marko opened the door to see the stocky demolition man he'd met at Grandma's. "It's you!"

"Who'd you expect? President Kallio?"

"But why would they send you?"

"The lieutenant had us finishing up a job in town, and he said you needed to be picked up." The man took off his cap when he saw Mother. "Pleased to meet you. I'm Pentti Jokinen, but the boys just call me Joki."

"The lieutenant promised that he would take good care—" Mother began.

"We'll watch him like he was our very own pup."
Joki clapped Marko on the shoulder.

"Marko, are you sure you want to do this?" Mother asked. "It's not too late to change your mind. You could help the soldiers just as much if you kept working in the hospital."

"I want to do my part at the front. Like everyone else."

"It would be so much safer here," Mother said. "All of Savolahti must be in ashes by now." Mother was crying even harder than she had at the train station.

"Remember, you've taught me well." Marko grabbed his pack.

"You promise to be careful?"

"I promise."

Mother kissed Marko's cheek and hugged him one last time. "Be safe."

Marko felt a jumble of emotions as he walked across the yard. He was excited, but at the same time he felt guilty for leaving Mother alone and frightened by what might lie ahead. He kept thinking back to the wounded soldier from Savolahti in the hospital. As bold as the young man's words had been, Marko had noticed a lost look in his eyes that made him uneasy.

Marko climbed into the rear of the sleigh, while Mother stood at the front gate, still crying. For an instant he thought about jumping back down. *My mother needs me*, he could say. *This was a crazy idea anyway. I'll just grab my pack and . . .*

"Goodbye," she called, waving. Marko's eyes filled with tears.

Joki's partner, Kekko, called from the front seat, "Welcome to the war, messenger boy." A cigarette stub stuck out of the corner of his mouth, and the broken chin strap of his helmet swung in the breeze.

Marko waved over his shoulder as Kekko picked up the reins and the matched pair of grays jerked the sleigh forward.

When Marko turned toward the front, Joki asked, "So where'd you get the gimpy leg?"

Marko blushed. He'd tried to hide his limp. "Polio a few years back."

"We don't care if you're gimpy if you can ski hard and shoot straight," Kekko said.

When the horses trotted past the west side of the church, Joki pointed at a weathered pole and a rusty chain and collar. "How'd you like to spend a day with your neck in that?"

"They call it the shaming pole," Marko said. "My grandma said they used to lock students in that iron collar if they didn't learn their catechism."

"The preacher in our village thought smarts could be knocked into a boy's head, too," Joki said.

"He tried it on me," Kekko said.

"And it never took!" Joki laughed and punched his shoulder.

Marko didn't laugh. He could imagine how the boys felt who'd been shackled there and taunted by their friends.

Before they started down the hill out of town, Marko looked back at the twin flags of Kronholm Castle and the church tower one last time. He would do everything he could to make the Russians pay for Johan's death.

Marko sat back and noticed a big coil of wire in the back of the sleigh. "Did you come to town for blasting wire?"

"We used most of it right here," Joki said.

"Doing what?" Marko asked.

"Rigging the bridge," Joki said.

"Not the Virtalinna bridge?" Marko said.

"Ain't no other bridge in town," Joki said.

"We got a charge on every piling," Kekko said.

"But the lieutenant said we need to hold the line in this sector," Marko said.

"We do," Joki said. "But a smart commander always has a backup plan. If the Russians breach our defenses, we got no choice but to torch this place and blow the bridge."

"Burn Virtalinna?"

"We'll stop those Russkies any way we can," Kekko said.

Marko pulled his coat tight around him. If Savolahti fell, Virtalinna and all the rest of Finland might be lost as well.

The road was in worse shape than on the day he'd driven to his grandmother's. When the sleigh lurched toward the ditch, Kekko grumbled, "How can a fellow run a rig with this skimpy covering of snow?"

"We could have took the wagon," Joki said.

"We'da busted an axle," Kekko said.

Every bump hurt Marko's leg, but he tried not to show it.

The roadside was littered with material abandoned by the army and the refugees. A broken wagon wheel lay beside a tin oil drum. A bedspring leaned against a stalled flatbed truck. Ammunition boxes were scattered over the ditch bank, along with a sewing machine, a suitcase, and a kitchen table with four chairs. At the edge of a swamp they passed a dead cow mired in the frozen mud.

At noon they met another sleigh and pulled over to let it pass. The wounded soldiers lying in back groaned every time the runners hit a bump.

Kekko flicked his cigarette away and pulled a canteen and a piece of hardtack out of his pack. "Want a bite?" he asked.

"My mother packed me a lunch," Marko said.

Kekko smiled at Joki.

"Let's see what sort of a cook your momma is, messenger boy," Joki said. "A good soldier always shares his grub."

"He always shares." Kekko shoved his hardtack back in his pack and held out his hand.

As Joki and Kekko chewed on Mother's fresh rye bread, Joki said, "Why don't you show him some of your tricks?"

"Naw," Kekko said.

"Does he do magic?" Marko asked.

"Lots better than that," Joki said. "Kekko can twist up

his face like nobody else. A magazine had a contest last winter. Kekko sent in his picture and won first place. Fifty marks! Just for making a face. Do that lip trick."

"All righty," Kekko said, swallowing the last of his bread.

Kekko stretched his bottom lip right up over the tip of his nose, and at the same time he crossed his eyes so tight that they looked right at each other.

Marko couldn't stop laughing.

"A rare talent!" Joki said.

Marko saw an approaching sleigh. "More wounded?"

Joki shook his head. "Those boys are scheduled for a train ride home."

As the sleigh runners hissed past, Marko was stunned to see a pile of dead Finnish soldiers. Their bodies were frozen in twisted positions and only partly covered by the canvas.

Joki was grim. "The first time Kekko and I saw a load like that we were on our way to the front, joking and singing patriotic songs."

"But we didn't sing no more after that." Kekko bit off a piece of Marko's cheese.

"Bodies freeze up real fast in the cold," Joki said. "One morning at first light a greenhorn emptied his clip into a Russkie sitting just beyond our trenches before he figured out the fellow was dead and frozen stiff."

Long after the sleigh had passed, the blue face of one dead soldier stayed in Marko's mind. The boy was about Marko's age. His eyes were open wide and his lashes were flecked with frost.

No older than me, Marko thought as the wagon bounced over a rut. *No older than Johan. And if there are so many dead coming from this battlefield . . . What about Father? Could he be lying in the back of a sleigh, cold and blue?*

"You finished with that bread?" Joki asked.

"What?" Marko shivered, still trying to blot out the face of the dead boy.

"I said, are you gonna eat that last hunk of bread?"

"Go ahead," Marko said.

"Suit yourself, messenger boy." Joki plucked the bread from Marko's hand. "But you can't be letting a little thing like a corpse put you off your feed. That's the way it is out here."

Kekko nodded. "Just the way it is."

CHAPTER 10

THE SOUP CANNON

An hour later, Kekko stopped the sleigh on the crest of a hill. "Quite a sight, ain't it?" he said. The sun was low in the sky.

Marko sat up. This couldn't be the road to his grandmother's village! The forest to their left was pockmarked with craters from artillery shells, and the snow was black. Trees tipped at odd angles, and boulders had been blasted to flinders. A dozen burned-out Russian tanks stood below the hill.

"The Russkies have been shelling us hard," Joki said.

"But we've held them back so far," Kekko said.

Marko saw a bonfire blazing at the edge of the woods south of the village. "Didn't you burn everything down?" he asked.

"That's a Russkie campfire," Joki said. "They huddle close to their fires at night."

"We're thinking they're short on tents," Kekko said.

"They make easy targets for our snipers in the dark," Joki said, "but once the sun comes up and they decide to charge, they're fearsome straight-ahead fighters."

"And you don't never want to get into a close-quarters fight with a Russkie," Kekko said. "They carry rattail bayonets that'll skewer you like a stuck pig."

"Where are all our men?" Marko asked.

"Companies One and Two are spread out along the back of this ridge," Joki said. "Their job is to keep the Russkies from pushing west. Our outfit is across the valley behind Horseshoe Hill. We stay hidden in the woods during the day so the Russkies' artillery can't zero in. At night we ski out in small groups and attack."

"Why is Company Three way over there?" Marko looked beyond the Russian campfires toward the dark hill.

"When the Russkies first advanced on Savolahti, we surprised them with a *motti* maneuver by skiing in wide circles through the woods and setting up behind them. Once we outflanked them, we split their column and chopped 'em to pieces. What's left of their regiment is trapped below."

North of the Russian camp Marko could see the charred ruins of Grandma's village. All the buildings had been burned except for the brick pottery factory and the mayor's house.

"The Russians didn't fall for your booby trap in the mayor's house," Marko said.

"We're still hoping," Kekko said as he started the sleigh down a logging road that led south through a stand of birch and aspen. Marko and Grandma had picked mushrooms there on a sunny day the previous fall.

The road gradually swung back to the east. When they started up a pine ridge on the backside of Horseshoe Hill, Marko noticed smoke drifting through the trees. "What's that from?"

"Our soup cannon," Joki said.

"You shoot soup at the Russians?" Marko asked.

"Ha, ha, ha," Kekko laughed, separating each *ha* from the next. "That's a good one."

"The soup cannon is our mobile field kitchen," Joki told Marko. "It's right under those spruce."

Marko saw a horse-drawn vat with a built-in wood-burning stove underneath it and a smokestack sticking out the top.

"Our tents are that way." Joki waved to his left. "The cooks keep their kitchen back here so the smoke don't draw artillery fire. Our squads ski over and eat one at a time."

"Ain't we gonna stop?" Kekko asked.

"Your dinner can wait until we deliver this boy to the lieutenant," Joki said.

A minute later they entered a thick spruce grove, and Joki said, "Here's Company Three."

"You'd never know a camp was here," Marko said. It was so dark that he had to squint to see the half dozen green tents, tucked under the spruce trees and camouflaged by the branches.

"That's the idea," Joki said. "We're out of sight back here, but our trenches and tank traps are dug in just a few hundred meters away on the front side of the hill. That first tent is our field hospital. The wounded they can't patch up are hauled to Virtalinna."

When Kekko pulled the horses to a stop, Joki jumped down and said, "I'll show Marko to the lieutenant's tent. You can unload the blasting wire. This way." Joki started down the snow-packed path. Marko slung his pack over his shoulder and hurried to catch up.

They walked past a soldier sitting on a log in front of the hospital tent and staring toward the woods. The man's face was so white that it took Marko a moment to realize he was a neighbor from Virtalinna.

"Eino, how are you?" Marko asked.

The man never blinked.

"It's me, Marko. Don't you recognize me?"

"Why did you come here?" Eino spoke in a slow, raspy voice, but he still stared straight ahead. It was the same lost look the soldier from Savolahti had had in the hospital, only a hundred times worse.

Joki patted Eino on the shoulder and said, "Hang in there, buddy." Then he led Marko away.

When they got behind the tent, Joki said, "We call that the thousand-yard stare. Eino is with our antitank squad. He's been like that since our last little fireworks."

"What caused it?" Marko asked as Joki kept walking.

"Nobody knows," Joki said. "He was in top form during the battle. He shoved a log into a tank track and stopped it single-handed. But when the Russkies pulled back we found him sitting on the ground staring. Our medic says when the brain takes in more than it can sort out, the eyes go blank sometimes."

"Will he get better?" Marko asked.

"No telling. The command tent is right up there." He pointed up the hill. "Let's see if the boss is in."

"Lieutenant?" Joki called as he stepped through the door of the twenty-man tent. "We've fetched your messenger boy."

Marko tried to hide his limp as he entered the eight-sided tent, but he couldn't keep his brace from clacking. An unlit stove stood in the middle of the tent, and the sleeping area was piled with spruce boughs, extra blankets, boots, and gas masks. A kerosene lantern hung from the center pole.

Marko's eyes tried to adjust to the dim light.

Juhola was kneeling on a blanket, studying a black and white map spread out over a rucksack. Two men looked over his shoulders. "Did we get the right boy?" Joki asked.

"You got the right man," the lieutenant said. He stood up and shook Marko's hand in a steel grip. "Welcome to the front."

Joki said, "I'll go help Kekko unload."

"Thanks, Joki," Juhola said.

The tent was so cold inside that frost coated the corners. The men had hung wet clothing from a line strung over the stove, and the air smelled of sweat, boot leather, and wet wool.

"I know it's cold in here, but we can only risk a fire at night," Juhola said. He turned to the rest of the men. "Meet my command group." The lieutenant used the same quiet voice as in the classroom, but Marko could tell that the men respected him. He pointed to a man in a neat uniform at his left. "This is Second Lieutenant Kerola, my assistant. Seppo and Juho are my observer patrol, and over in the corner are Niilo and Karl, my messengers."

The men nodded at Marko. No one spoke.

Marko studied the weary faces of the soldiers. Half the men had coughs and runny noses, and their wool pants and suspenders made them look more like farmers than soldiers. The exception was Kerola, whose shiny boots and neat green jacket were straight from military school.

Karl was about Marko's age. His Civil Guard uniform was too big, and he'd pulled a stocking hat down to his eyebrows. Spiky blond hair stuck out from under his cap, and his eyes were a deep blue. Marko was glad to see that he'd be working with at least one young person.

"Karl," the lieutenant said, "why don't you bring Marko to the supply tent to get his whiteovers and skis? Then he'll be ready for duty in the morning."

"Will do."

When Marko turned to leave the tent, his leg brace creaked.

"What's that squeaking?" Seppo asked. He had a coarse brown beard. He wore smudged glasses with black tape across the bridge, and he blinked constantly.

Seppo set down the sniper rifle that he'd been cleaning and walked over to Marko. He bent down and tapped the toe of Marko's boot. "You got springs in there?"

"I have a leg brace." Marko had hoped to keep it a secret.

Seppo lifted the bottom of Marko's pant leg and saw the metal slats that supported his ankle. "Would you look at that? We got us a mechanical boy!"

The other men laughed.

"Marko caught polio a few years back," the lieutenant said. "But he hasn't let it slow him up."

"Let's hope he can ski." Seppo blinked his weasel eyes.

Karl stepped outside, and Marko hurried to catch up. He asked Karl, "Are you from around here?"

"Tervola," Karl said, keeping his head down as he walked toward the supply tent.

"The village north of here?" Marko asked.

Instead of answering, Karl studied Marko's limp. "How can you deliver messages with a bum leg?"

"I ski just fine."

Karl shook his head as though he didn't believe it, and he didn't say another word the whole way to the supply tent.

CHAPTER 11

SPARK DUTY

Marko lay in the dark tent, half awake, thinking back on a hot June day when he and Johan had gone bog-walking through a swamp north of Grandma's farm.

"Come on, slowpoke," Johan had called over his shoulder. He and Marko had strapped on special, ten-foot-long skis, and they were headed for an abandoned hermit's cabin that stood on a ridge in the middle of the swamp.

"I thought you said the swamp would be no problem." Marko looked down at his muddy pants as he balanced on a mossy hummock to avoid a pool of water.

Johan was soaked to his knees, but he remained cheerful. "This is even better! I'll bet nobody's made it out here in years."

Marko slapped a mosquito on his neck.

When they finally got to the cabin, it was empty ex- cept for a few cracked dishes and rusty tools. The moss-covered roof looked ready to collapse, and the floor creaked dangerously.

"Let's go," Marko said.

Johan had knelt down and was pulling a small wooden chest from under the bed. "Look at this!" he shouted.

"Wow!" Marko ran over.

But when Johan lifted the lid, all they saw was a stack of handwritten sheet music.

"Every note is perfectly drawn." Johan studied a sheet. "If only we could read music."

"Who cares?" Marko started for the doorway.

"But what if this old guy was some sort of Sibelius, living out here by himself and writing masterpieces?"

"Let's go," Marko said.

Johan closed the lid, and they left all the music behind. But ever since that day Marko had always wished they'd brought a few sheets to their music teacher.

"Wake up, Gimpy."

Marko turned with a start. Juho was crouched beside him, smelling of stale tobacco.

"Time for spark duty," Juho said. He had a pasty complexion and his blond beard was stained with tobacco juice.

"What?"

"It's your turn to tend the fire," Juho said. "Make

sure it don't go out. And watch for embers landing on the roof and sparks jumping out of the stove. The wood-pile's out back."

As Juho lay down, he added, "Since you're a green-horn, you got double spark duty. Wake Karl after your two hours is up."

Juho was soon snoring. Marko sat up and yawned. The different pitches and the wheezing of the snorers had made it hard for him to get to sleep. The noisiest fellow was in the far corner. He sucked in each breath with a long whistle that sounded like someone inflating a truck tire. Then he held his breath so long that Marko thought he'd died before he let it out with a big, lip-flapping whoosh.

Someone had set their rotten boots beside Marko's blanket, and another terrible smell came from the socks and foot rags on the clothesline above the stove. The foot rags were soft pieces of flannel cloth that the sol-diers wrapped around their feet before they slipped on their boots. They could be dried out quickly over a fire or by hanging them on a tree branch.

Marko pulled out his watch and tilted the face so he could read it in the red glow of the stove. Pale moonlight filtered through the canvas roof. It was two o'clock. How could he ever stay awake until four?

Marko rubbed his calf to ease the stabbing pain. He wasn't used to wearing his brace at night, but everyone slept in their clothes, and he knew the men would tease him if he took it off.

The sharp ache reminded Marko of his first days in

the hospital. He'd sweated so much that he lost twenty pounds in two weeks. Mother held a cool washcloth to his forehead and told him to block the pain by thinking about something peaceful. He always imagined the last day his leg had been normal.

He and Johan had spent the afternoon swimming in the lake. They'd sunned themselves on an island and were swimming back to shore when a loon surfaced only a few meters in front of them. The loon called, and Marko answered with a silly, laughing cry. When the loon dove, the boys dove, too. Marko opened his eyes under water and swam toward the bird, but all he saw were tall green weeds and white sand. When Marko and Johan came up, the loon was laughing right behind them. Each time the boys dove, the loon played the same trick. After they swam to shore and toweled themselves off, the loon called one last time. Then he slipped under the water and disappeared.

Now Marko stood up, stretched his leg, and stepped over the man next to him to check the stove. The intake plate rattled as the fire pulled in air, and the lid fit so poorly that smoke leaked out. The stovepipe ran through a piece of metal flashing in the roof, and it looked as if one spark could set the tent on fire.

Marko slipped on his coat and stepped outside to get more wood. A three-quarter moon hung above the black pines. The light sparkling on the snow made it nearly as bright as day. As he breathed in wood smoke mingled with cold, piney air, he thought of Mother. *She'll have to carry her own firewood now.*

"What's the password?" a voice snapped.

Marko turned. A rifle pointed at his chest. "Ahh!" *What, what is the password Kerola told me?*

"You're lucky it's my night for guard duty." Joki stepped out of the shadows. "Some of these boys woulda shot you dead."

"*Sekahedelmäkeitto.*" Marko remembered the word. "Fruit soup!"

"If you want to live to have another bowl," Joki said, "don't forget the password."

As Marko's eyes adjusted to the moonlight, he saw the path to the woodpile. He'd just loaded his arms when he saw a red flash in the west. Then he heard a faint whizzing.

"Is that you, Joki?" he asked, thinking it might be the demo man whistling. It almost sounded like a bomb, but Marko hadn't heard a plane. The whiz turned to a high-pitched howl.

Marko looked up as an artillery shell ripped through the top of a spruce tree. Branches snapped off, snow flew in all directions, and the shell exploded with a deafening boom.

Shrapnel zinged through the trees, slicing off hunks of bark and ricocheting off boulders. Marko ducked as frozen clods of dirt and pieces of rock rained down.

"Attack!" Marko yelled, rushing back and pulling open the tent door. "The Russians are attacking!"

The lieutenant lifted his head. "Take it easy, Koski."

"It's artillery. We—" Marko stopped. Why wasn't everyone jumping up and putting on their boots?

"Listen to your lieutenant." Juho's voice was slow and sleepy. "They lob a shell over the hill now and then just to rile us up. Don't get your underwear in a bundle over it."

With that Juho went back to snoring.

CHAPTER 12

SPECIAL DELIVERY

"You gonna sleep all day?"

Marko opened his eyes and squinted in the yellow light of the kerosene lamp. Karl and Niilo were looking down at him. It took him a moment to remember where he was.

Second Lieutenant Kerola handed a packet to Niilo. "As soon as Marko's up, you fellows get going."

Marko threw off his blanket and scrambled to pull on his boots. When his leg brace creaked, Juho said, "Our mechanical man needs some oiling."

Marko's face burned as the men laughed.

"And he don't know how to get dressed without his momma." Seppo blinked and pushed his glasses up on his nose. He fingered the dog tags that Marko had been issued the day before. "These death tags go under your shirt." He stuffed them down Marko's neck.

"How else we gonna know who you are if the Russkies blow your head off?" Juho laughed.

Marko put on his new whiteovers. The pants fit, but the coat was so big that the hood hung down over his face.

"Ha, ha," Seppo said. "Gimpy is blind now, too."

"Let's see how your helmet fits." Niilo bent to pick it up. Niilo was the shortest man Marko had ever seen. His skin was dark, and his bushy eyebrows gave him the look of a bear.

Marko pulled back his hood, and Niilo plunked the helmet on his head. When it covered up his eyes, Niilo said, "Nah. Too big. You've got to see where you're ski-ing. Just wear your cap."

Juhola finished shaving, using his helmet as a wash-basin. The other men in the command group had scrag-gly beards, but he looked as neat as he had in the classroom. He turned to Marko as he toweled off his face. "We normally send messengers out in pairs, but I want Niilo and Karl to show you the ropes today."

He pitched his wash water out the door and nodded to Niilo. "You know the routine. I'm taking Kahvi over to check on the First Platoon." He dried the inside of his helmet, put the liner back in, and grabbed his coat. "Report to the command trench when you get back."

As Juhola left the tent, Marko was confused. *Kahvi* was the word for coffee. "Why would the lieutenant need coffee to check on a platoon?"

"Kahvi is the name of his horse," Karl said.

The moon still hung in the predawn sky when the messengers stepped outside. Niilo said, "We got backwoods trails that lead to the other companies."

Niilo wore high brown ski boots that had curled-up toes. "Where'd you get those?" Marko asked.

"Made them myself out of reindeer hide. They slide in and out of bindings better than those farm boots of yours. Us Laplanders live on skis." He stepped into his skis and started down the trail.

Karl said, "We don't have all day," and followed Niilo.

Though Marko could barely see in the gray light, he threw on his pack and hurried to catch up. He'd only taken a few strides when a branch slapped across his face and cut his lip.

He and Johan had always held back branches and looked out for each other on the trail, but Marko saw he would have to be on his guard out here.

They'd only covered a couple of hundred meters when Niilo coasted to a stop. "We'll catch some breakfast here."

Hidden at the edge of the woods stood the field kitchen. The cook said, "You're running behind today."

"We got us a late sleeper," Karl said. He and Niilo slipped off their packs and opened their mess kits. The cook ladled a scoop of rye porridge onto the lower part of each kit and filled the lid with tea.

Juho and Seppo were already eating. "Tea is for pansies," Seppo said. He poured himself coffee from a blackened pot beside the coals and took a big drink without checking to see if it was hot.

"Hey! Didn't you burn your mouth?" Karl asked.

Juho laughed. "Seppo drinks straight from the pot when we're in a hurry."

Seppo wiped his face on his sleeve. "Strong coffee helps me see my rifle sights when I'm hunting Russkies."

Marko had only taken two spoonfuls of porridge when he saw that Niilo and Karl had already wolfed theirs down. They swigged down their tea and washed their mess kits in the snow. Marko gobbled his breakfast and cleaned his kit while Niilo filled his canteen with tea and put a few squares of *näkkileipä,* a hard rye bread, into his mess kit bag. "You'd better grab some, too."

Niilo started up a trail that led north. "Company One is this way," he said. "Keep your eyes peeled for Russkie scouts."

Marko skied hard to keep up. Niilo's arms pumped like a machine, and Karl, who had longer legs than Marko, was a good skier as well.

The sun was beginning to filter through the pine tops when the trail swung west. In the distance Marko could see a long ridge overlooking the valley. Suddenly Niilo and Karl stopped. Marko had to tip his ski edges outward to keep from running up the back of Karl's skis.

"Those rascals got what they deserved." Niilo stared into a swale.

Three Russian soldiers lay dead in the snow.

"They tried to sneak behind our lines two nights

ago"—Karl spat into the snow—"but our patrol caught them."

The brown uniforms were covered with thick frost. A dark beard showed on the chin of one man. His eye sockets were filled with snow, and his boots were missing.

"Sooner or later the Russkies will all get their medals plucked," Niilo said.

"Our men took their medals?" Marko asked.

"They make great souvenirs," Karl said.

Marko shook his head. "Who would steal a dead man's boots?"

Karl looked down. "My feet are pretty small, so I was lucky when Juho brought me these. They're a whole lot better than the old manure kickers I wore on the farm."

"But my Civil Guard instructors said that soldiers should respect the enemy dead."

"It's easy to preach when you're safe and warm in a classroom," Karl said. "Out here it's everyone for himself."

The bitterness in Karl's voice chilled Marko.

"Let's go." Niilo planted his poles and kicked forward.

On the way to Company One, Niilo and Karl filled Marko in on what his job would be like. Field telephones connected Companies One and Two, but Company Three, which was seven kilometers away, relied on messengers. "It's just as well we hand-deliver," Niilo said,

" 'cause the Russkies splice into phone lines and eaves-drop."

When it was time to ski back to camp, Niilo stopped at the head of the trail and took off his whiteovers and his jacket. Then he peeled off his shirt and undershirt! Steam rose off his hairy back as he reached into his pack. Was he crazy?

Niilo said, "Best to swap shirts when you get sweaty." He shoved his damp undershirt into his pack and pulled a dry one over his head. "You're chilly for a minute, but it helps in the long run."

Marko looked at Karl, but Niilo shook his head. "He won't try it. He don't believe this old Laplander knows about winter."

Marko stripped to his waist, but by the time he had his new shirt and coat back on, his whole body was shaking. "This is nuts," he said, his teeth chattering.

"Grab your ski poles," Niilo said. "You got to move fast."

Marko vowed he was never going to do such a stupid thing again. But partway up the next hill his shivering stopped.

"How you doing now?" Niilo called over his shoulder.

"Warmer," Marko said. "And drier."

Niilo stopped on the crest of the ridge and turned to Marko. "Us reindeer people know how to live with cold."

"You sure do! So—how often do we carry messages?" Marko asked.

"Sometimes we go a day or two without a run," Niilo said.

"But on a busy day we might make three trips," Karl put in.

"What do we do when there's no deliveries?" Marko asked.

"What do you think we do? Tie silver bells on our sleigh and ride to the nearest manor house for tea?" Karl asked. "There's plenty of little jobs in camp."

Niilo grinned as Karl pushed past Marko and started down the trail. "Karl don't like to waste time on small talk."

CHAPTER 13

A COCKTAIL FOR
COMRADE MOLOTOV

Marko's leg was throbbing by the time the messengers reported to the command trench, but he wasn't about to let anyone know. One day, after Marko had passed Johan at the finish line in a ski race, Johan asked, "What makes you push so hard?"

"It started on the day the doctor told my mother that I wouldn't ever walk and play like a normal boy."

"So you're still working to prove him wrong?"

"Every day of my life," Marko said.

The command trench was dug into the hillside and concealed by a berm of earth, logs, and spruce boughs. Narrow exit trenches on both ends allowed the men to stay hidden as they moved up to the camp or down to the battlefield. The elevation offered a view of the woods where the Russians were camped and the no-man's-land between.

Juhola was briefing two platoon leaders, who turned and looked at Marko.

"Meet Marko Koski," the lieutenant said. "A student of mine from Virtalinna." Marko nodded politely at the men.

The soldier beside Kerola spoke. "Is he the one Seppo calls Gimpy?"

Everyone laughed except for a square-shouldered sergeant, who extended his hand. "Pleased to meet you, son," he said. "I'm Henri Hauta, the fellow who's in charge of those loony cases Joki and Kekko. Folks call me Hoot." Hoot had a thick neck and a broad face, and his hand was as big as a shovel. He reminded Marko of Grandma's saying, "Finns are the toughest bulls in the pasture."

Marko rarely met a man stronger than his father, but when Hoot pumped Marko's arm, Marko's feet nearly rose off the ground. Hoot stopped and said, "Hey! Where'd a city boy get a strong grip like that?"

"My father is a blacksmith. I help him at the forge."

"Iron men make good soldiers," Hoot said, clapping Marko on the shoulder and nearly knocking him over.

Kerola took the communication packet from Niilo, and the lieutenant turned back to the map that he'd covered with tracing paper. "This is the sector we need to watch. If they move, we'll have two choices—"

A voice hollered from up the hill, "Where's them messenger boys?"

When Joki appeared, Kerola said, "Can't you see we've got a meeting going on here?"

"It's all right, Mr. Kerola," the lieutenant said. "I told Joki he could borrow Karl and Marko."

Joki waved at the boys. "This way, pups."

"I know what Joki's got planned for them," Seppo said.

"Mixing cocktails." Juho grinned.

As they walked up the hill, Joki whispered, "Don't pay no attention to Kerola. He's a career man. Like all the lifers, he's using this war to hunt for a promotion."

But Marko was frowning over what Juho had said. "What did he mean, mixing cocktails?"

"You're going to help us toast our friend Comrade Molotov," Joki said. "Time's a-wasting." He led them past the tents to a sleigh filled with cases of empty vodka bottles.

"Welcome to our party." Kekko walked up with a gasoline can in his hand. A cigarette dangled from his lower lip.

Kekko picked up a vodka bottle filled with amber goo. "This here container was manufactured by the Koskenkorva vodka factory. But I wouldn't recommend taking a nip unless you have a taste for kerosene and tar. Once we add a shot of gasoline, we'll have a first-rate antitank weapon. They normally come ready-made, but our last shipment got held up."

"You blow up tanks with liquor bottles?" Marko said.

"We'd rather use antitank guns," Joki said.

"But we've never had any," Kekko said.

"And antitank mines are in short supply," Joki said.

"Don't you have to get really close with those bottles?" Marko asked.

"Depends on how good your pitching arm is," Joki said. "But once you sneak inside ten meters the tanks can't see you anyway."

"That's assuming your head's still attached," Kekko said.

"Then we light the wick and throw for the air vent," Joki said.

"*Kaboom!* Roasted Russians!" Kekko set the bottle on the plank that he'd laid across the back of the sleigh. "Pay attention and I'll show you our private recipe."

Karl grumbled, "Do I have to listen to all this again?"

"Mind your manners," Kekko said. "Now—you hold the bottle so it don't tip. Then you put the funnel in the neck like so." He reached for the gasoline can and started pouring.

Marko asked, "So you named these bombs after the Russian foreign minister, Molotov?"

"The very same pig," Kekko said.

"Molotov and Stalin are the ones who started this war," Joki said. "And we aim to give them a proper thank-you."

Kekko corked the bottle and smiled. "One down, six dozen to go." He held up the bomb and jiggled the black and amber contents. "Ain't she pretty?" His cigarette ashes fell onto his pant leg.

"Watch that cigarette!" Marko said.

"These bottles is harmless without a wick," Kekko said.

Marko was ready to run if the gas caught on fire, but Karl took the bomb from Kekko. "Too bad we can't shove this one down Molotov's throat." It was the first time Marko had seen Karl smile.

Joki said, "We should recruit you for our antitank squad."

"I like Karl's mean streak," Kekko said.

Marko asked Joki, "Will the Russians attack soon?"

"No telling. Two days ago they hit Companies One and Two hard. We joke about them, but once the lead starts flying they're mighty tough fighters."

"I thought there'd be constant gunfire on the front," Marko said.

"I used to think wars was all shooting, too," Joki said. "But battlefields are mainly quiet. Out here we wait until we can't stand it. Then we wait some more."

"That's the army," Kekko said. "Hurry up and wait."

"The fireworks can start up any second," Joki said, "but guessin' when only makes it harder. I do know the Russkies are making a big mistake by not hammering us in this warm weather."

"The lieutenant said the same thing," Marko said.

"They should know winter makes us Finns tougher."

"The colder the better," Kekko said.

"By the feel of that wind"—Joki looked to the north—"a front will be moving in soon."

"You pups ready to spill some gasoline?" Kekko asked.

As Joki handed Karl the funnel, Juho and Seppo skied by with rifles on their shoulders. "Looks like Gimpy found a job he can handle," Seppo shouted.

Marko's ears burned under his cap.

"Watch me run like Gimpy," Juho said. Stepping out of his skis, he jogged a few meters, swinging his leg out to one side.

After they left, Karl asked, "Where are they headed tonight?"

"Hard to tell," Joki said. "Those observers are ghosts who favor night patrols. They might stay here in the valley. Or they might ski twenty kilometers behind enemy lines to spy."

Though filling the bottles was smelly work, Marko knew he'd rather be stuck making bombs with crabby Karl than have to sneak into Russian territory in the dark.

By the time they'd corked their last Molotov cocktail, Marko had a headache from the gas and kerosene fumes. But Karl looked happy.

"How many tanks can you blow up with these?" Karl asked.

"Antitank work is a bit of skill mixed in with a bunch of luck," Kekko said. "Truth is we're more likely to blow ourselves up than kill a tank."

When Kekko left, Marko asked Karl, "How come you hate the Russians so much?"

"Don't you?"

"They killed my best friend, and my father was called back to active duty, but I—"

"Two more reasons they deserve to die." Karl walked away.

CHAPTER 14

THE WOODPILE AND
THE FOXHOLE

"Mailman!" a voice called just before lunch the next day. A man stepped inside the tent and asked, "Marko Koski here?"

"That's me."

"Package for you." He tossed Marko a fat parcel tied with string. "I'm not the regular mailman. I usually make the hospital run, and your mother asked me to drop this off."

Inside, a letter from Mother was tucked on top of a bundle of clothing.

Dear Marko,

I hope this letter finds you well. Every day I tell myself that you made the right decision in going to the front, but it doesn't ease my worries. Remind the lieutenant of his promise!

The good news is that Grandma and the children arrived safely in Sweden. We are busier than ever here at the hospital. The rationing program is getting stricter these days. Not only do we need coupons for coffee, sugar, gas, butter, and other commodities, but the government has also added cloth to the list. They want people to use paper sheets! Can you imagine sleeping on paper? The ladies in town knitted these clothes for anyone in your unit who can use them. We are treating men for frostbite already, so I know you need warm things out there.

Seppo squinted over Marko's shoulder. "Did Marko get a letter from his mommy telling him not to wet his pants when the Russkies attack?"

"My mother and her friends sent these for our company." Marko pointed to the pile of hats, neck warmers, gloves, and socks, all different colors and sizes.

"Where's that messenger boy?" Kekko entered the tent. "We heard you got a package from home." Kekko looked at the pile. "Only clothes? None of your momma's good bread?" He peered under the bundle and his grin got even bigger. "A tin, I see." He pulled it out and rattled it. "If these are cookies, will you be shar-ing with your good buddy Kekko?"

"Don't you want to wait until after lunch?" Marko teased.

Kekko shook his head. "I always say life is no sure thing, so eat your dessert first."

Marko grinned. "So pass the cookies around!"

After lunch Marko learned what Karl meant by "lit-tle jobs" when Kerola snapped, "The supply sergeant wants you boys on firewood detail this afternoon."

Karl led Marko to a clearing behind the hospital tent where the teamsters had skidded in a pile of tree-length birch. A two-man crosscut saw and an axe leaned against a sawbuck.

"We've got to cut the pieces real short for that tent stove and split 'em small because the wood's so green," Karl said.

After they'd sawed up a pile of wood, Marko looked at the axe. The edge was dull and pitted. "My father al-ways says, 'A sharp axe spares the back.' You suppose the supply sergeant would have a file?"

Karl shrugged. Marko said, "I'll go see."

Marko returned with a file and set the axe head on the sawbuck. After he sharpened one side, he held up the blade.

Karl complained, "We could've split half the wood by now."

Marko turned the blade over and filed the other side. "My father's a blacksmith, and—"

"Who cares what your father says?"

Marko set the axe down. He was getting tired of Karl's grumpiness. "Hasn't your father ever given you advice?"

"My father's dead," Karl said.

"I thought your brother was dead."

"He is." Karl's voice was flat. "And so are my father, my mother, and my sister."

"But how?"

"The Russians killed them on the first morning of the war. Our farm was right on the border. My father ignored the evacuation warnings. Because my mother was Russian, he thought we'd be safe."

Now Marko understood Karl's anger. "I'm sorry," Marko said. "Real sorry. I didn't mean to—"

"I'll split and you pile," Karl said, standing a piece of birch on end. "Then we can trade places."

Karl hefted the axe. With a sharp thwack the birch split in two. Karl looked at the blade. "That edge makes a difference."

After splitting and piling wood all afternoon, Marko was hoping for a message run. Instead, the supply sergeant said, "I'm switching you boys to foxhole detail. A teamster will show you what we need done."

The man led them to a low area out of the wind behind Horseshoe Hill. "This is what we got done so far." He pointed to a shallow, eight-foot-long trench.

"I thought foxholes held only one soldier," Marko
said.

"They do," the teamster said, "but this isn't for a soldier. It's for a horse. We need to go down another two meters."

"Two meters!" Marko said.

"I'm glad your ears work. When the shelling starts we need to get the animals under cover. There are your tools." He pointed to a pick and shovel. "See you boys at supper."

Marko stepped into the trench and tested the soil with the pick. The steel tip clanked against the frozen ground.

"It's hard work," Karl said, "but the horses deserve protection. Once we finish the hole, the teamsters will build a frame and cover it with boughs."

"You've dug these before?"

"I've helped with a couple," Karl said. "And I worked on the main stable—the one with the pole and canvas roof."

"Do you have horses at home?" Marko asked. He swung the pick, and his teethed jarred when he hit a frozen rock.

"I don't have a home no more," Karl said.

"Sorry," Marko said, wondering if he'd ever find a subject that didn't bring sorrow to Karl.

CHAPTER 15

THE SAUNA TENT

Marko woke to the sound of a hacking cough. Many soldiers had colds, and the sneezing and coughing made it hard to sleep. Marko tried not to groan as he sat up. The muscles in his back and arms were tight from splitting wood and digging. And the skin on his leg was raw. He wanted to take off his brace at night, but he wasn't about to let Juho and Seppo tease him. If the work was this hard, would he have the strength to keep up?

The sky was still black when Marko and Karl walked back to the trench. After digging by lantern light for an hour, Marko took off his mitts and stuck his hands under his jacket to warm them. "Why do you suppose the Russian army attacked your farm?"

"It wasn't like that." Karl leaned on his pick. "The

infantry stormed past our place before dawn. But at milking time a couple of stragglers showed up. They were small men with slimy-looking eyes. I'll never forget those eyes." Karl paused, and it seemed as if he was about to say more. Then he tossed down the pick. "We're gonna need a pry bar for this rock."

The more Marko worked with Karl, the more he missed Johan. Johan would have found a way to make trench digging fun by telling jokes or stories. But with Karl it was just pick and shovel all day long.

When Marko and Karl were walking back to the command tent at suppertime, the lieutenant rode up. His horse was lathered and his whiteovers were stained with soot and sweat. "Evening, gentlemen." He dismounted. "Karl, would you take Kahvi to the stable for me?" He handed Karl the reins.

After Karl had left, Juhola asked, "Is everything going all right with you and Karl?"

"We're getting to know each other," Marko said.

"Something's gnawing at him, and I was hoping you'd be able to help. If anyone knows how to bounce back from a rough place, you do."

Marko smiled. He'd never imagined that his teacher admired his courage.

"I'll do my best," Marko said. *But how can I help a boy who refuses to talk?*

By the time the squad had finished supper, a cold wind was blowing out of the north. Back at the tent,

Marko started a letter to Mother. *Things are quiet here,* he began, thinking of words that might ease her worries.

Hoot Hauta, the antitank squad leader, stuck his bald head through the door. "Who's ready for a sauna?" Hoot had stripped to his long underwear but was still wearing his boots. Joki stood behind him, dwarfed by Hoot's broad shoulders.

"I forgot it was time for our Saturday-night bath," Juhola said. "We wouldn't miss it."

"The fire's hot," Joki said.

"And I fixed your watch." Hoot handed him a gold watch.

"Thanks, Hoot," the lieutenant said.

As Hoot walked off, Niilo noticed Marko staring. "You wouldn't think Hoot could work on something so small with those big meat hooks of hands. But he's a genius at fixing things. Give him a radio, a car engine, or a Suomi submachine gun and he'll break it down and put it back together before you can blink."

"You have a sauna out here in the woods?" Marko said.

"Hoot's squad rigged one up."

Everyone except Karl stripped to their long underwear, grabbed a towel, and followed the lieutenant out the door.

"Aren't you coming?" Marko asked Karl.

"It's too cold," Karl said.

"The kid never takes a sauna," Niilo said. "If his name wasn't Kangas, I wouldn't believe he was a Finn."

Outside, the stars were white and huge. The wind blew through Marko's underwear, making him shiver.

Behind the stable Marko saw smoke billowing from a red-hot stovepipe sticking through a canvas roof. The corners of the building were unpeeled spruce poles and the walls were piled boughs and stretched canvas. The door was a canvas flap.

From the inside Kekko lifted the flap. He held a water dipper in his left hand, and he was naked except for his dog tags. "We've got her cooking tonight!"

The hot air smelled of spruce needles and birch smoke. A wooden water bucket stood beside the stove, and a pail of rocks heated on top. The seats were ammunition crates. As the men took off their boots and hung their underwear on a clothesline, Kekko said, "Watch for slivers as you sit yourselves." Then he doused the rocks with a dipperful of water, and hot steam rushed up.

"Steam us up good," Joki said, picking something off his underwear shirt and flicking it at the stove. "I've got to kill off some of these bedbugs and lice before they chew me up."

Marko was glad that Juho and Seppo weren't there as he slipped off his brace and took a seat.

"Feels just like home, don't it?" Hoot said to Marko.

"Reminds me of the sauna at my grandma's farm."

"Did she have a smoke sauna?" Hoot tossed another dipperful on the rocks.

Marko nodded.

"I love the charred smell of those old-timey saunas," Hoot said, leaning back and closing his eyes.

The steam mingling with the smoke stirred up memories of summers at Grandma's. Marko and his father always helped her at haying time. After a day working with the men in the fields, nothing felt better than to sit on the cedar bench in the sauna and steam off the dust. Then everyone dove into the river.

Back on those hazy summer days Marko had never imagined that he'd be sitting in a crude sauna like this in the middle of the woods. As the heat soothed his sore muscles, he thought of the letter he would write to Mother if he could be honest:

> *We are camped in a cold forest at a place called Horseshoe Hill. I spend my days digging holes in the frozen ground with a boy who refuses to talk. The skin under my brace is blistered and bleeding, and I don't know how much longer I'll be able to stand it. I've seen the power of the Red Army artillery, and I shake every time I hear the whistle of an incoming shell. If the Russians ever pinpoint our location, those big guns will reduce my company to ashes.*

CHAPTER 16

A BLOODRED SKY

Marko breathed in the steam of the sauna, and everyone sat back and relaxed except Kekko. He leaned toward the lieutenant and asked, "Would you tell us about the time you went to the Olympics with Paavo Nurmi?"

"Most folks like it quiet in a sauna," Juhola said.

"I don't like it quiet nowhere," Kekko said. "I could show the boys a face-pulling trick to liven things up." He sucked in his cheeks and began rolling his lips over his teeth.

"How about that Paavo Nurmi story, Lieutenant?" Hoot asked.

Juhola smiled. "It was the summer of 1924. The Olympics were in Paris that year. I'd missed qualifying, but I traveled with the team. Paavo was in the best form of his life. He made the finals in both the fifteen-hundred- and five-thousand-meter races. He could have qualified for the ten thousand as well, but the Finnish Olympic team decided he was running in too many races."

"No fair," Kekko said, pouring water on the rocks.

"To make matters worse, the French scheduled the finals of the fifteen hundred and the five thousand only thirty minutes apart. Our coaches protested, but the judges only added a few more minutes.

"After winning the gold in the fifteen hundred meters, Paavo had to start the five thousand less than an hour later. He looked strong for the first two laps, checking his pace with his stopwatch like he always did. We figured he'd fade, but when he got to the final lap, he tossed down his watch and left everyone in the dust. The stadium exploded. The French did everything they could to make him lose, but he willed himself to win."

"I don't know much about track racing, but you'd think the Russkies would've heard of Paavo Nurmi and figured they'd have a fight on their hands when they started a war with us Finns." Hoot shook his head.

"Stalin planned on a quick march to Helsinki," the lieutenant said. "But you boys have shown the same toughness that Paavo did."

"You can count on us to—" Joki stopped when a huge explosion echoed up from the valley.

"What on earth?" Niilo said.

"I'll bet this cold wave finally convinced them Russkies to move into the mayor's house!" Kekko shouted.

Joki slapped his shoulder. "They found that little housewarming present we shoved up the chimney!"

"I can see their faces," Kekko said, making everyone roar as he pantomimed a Russian soldier warming his hands in front of the fireplace and then looking up the chimney. "Let's celebrate with a cool-down."

"Too bad we can't chop a hole in the river," Niilo said.

With a yell Kekko lifted up the canvas and dove into a snowbank. The rest of the men followed. As Marko rolled in the snow, his skin prickled all over. He watched steam rise off the bodies of the men. It felt so good to be clean.

"Holy St. Henry!" Joki tilted his head back. "Take a gander at that."

Marko looked up. The northern lights blazed above the trees. But instead of the usual wispy trails of green, the sky was streaked with red. The black pine tops were backlit by the bloodred fire, and flecks of starlight burned above.

"I'm not one to believe in curses," Joki said, "but it scares me to think what that bloody sky might mean."

"It probably means your chimney bomb just blew a good chunk of the Red Army straight to heaven," the lieutenant said.

"Ain't none of those Red devils going to heaven," Kekko said.

"As if you've got a place reserved for yourself up-stairs," Joki said, and the men all laughed.

CHAPTER 17

THE WRATH OF GOD

When Marko woke the next morning, he was sleepy from another night of double spark duty.

"Cold today." Marko eyed the thick frost in the corners of the tent.

Niilo was already dressed. "It's about time we had real winter."

"This weather will test the Russians," Juhola told them, pulling on his coat. "I'm off to the command trench. You boys check in down there after breakfast."

The messengers stepped outside and heard a far-off whistling. The noise rose to a higher pitch, like the air rushing from a giant bonfire. "Down!" Niilo yelled over the screech, and they all dove into the snow.

The shell exploded at the base of a nearby pine.
Marko covered his head as chunks of dirt and rock rained down. The tree shivered and crashed to the ground. Marko's ears rang from the concussion, and his heart pounded.

When the next two shells exploded down the ridge, Niilo stood up. "They're aiming at the forward trenches now."

Marko lifted his head and smiled.

"What are you gawking at?" Karl asked.

"Where'd you get that haircut?"

Karl's blond hair was plastered down, except for a few sawed-off clumps that stuck straight up. His forehead was white from being covered up by his hat, and his blue eyes looked huge.

"Let's get breakfast." Karl slapped his stocking hat on his leg to knock off the snow, then pulled it down over his ears.

Instead of stopping after a few rounds, as the shells had last time, the Russian artillery thundered all morning long. Each time a shell screamed toward the command trench, Marko swore it was going to be a direct hit. The explosions were twice as loud as they'd been in the woods, forcing the lieutenant to shout his orders. Smoke and dust burned Marko's eyes and throat.

While Niilo relayed messages to the forward trenches, Marko and Karl helped the medics use *pulkkas* or sleds to drag the wounded soldiers up the hill to the hospital tent. The slope made the pull difficult, and the chunks of rock and dirt that had been blasted over the snow forced the boys to lift the sleds over the roughest spots. The first two soldiers had minor shrapnel wounds, but the third man had been hit in the chest. Before the boys lifted him onto the sled, the medic gave him a shot of morphine. Despite the painkiller the man kept screaming.

"Hang on. We'll get you to the doc," Marko said, panting as he and Karl skidded the sled past a muddy crater and a splintered pine tree. Each time they bumped a root or a rock the man's screams stabbed Marko. "Hurry," he whispered to Karl. "We've got to hurry." Marko's head pounded. All the blood and the squealing reminded him of a pig-killing on his farm.

Once they carried the man inside the hospital tent, the head medic pulled back the soldier's dressing and shook his head. "He'll be ready for the cooling tent soon," he said softly. Then he moved on to the next patient.

When the boys started back down the hill, Marko asked, "What's the cooling tent?"

"That's where they keep the bodies," Karl said.

Marko stopped. "They're just going to let him die?"

"They help the ones who have a chance," Karl said.

"What if that was your bro—" Marko stopped. *Don't mention family.*

Karl was about to answer Marko when a soldier came staggering toward the hospital tent. "Oh my God," Karl said.

The soldier's right arm had been blown off above the elbow.

The boys ran to help him.

The guns were still booming when the messengers stopped for a lunch of dry rye bread and cold tea. The cooks had doused their fire in case a Russian advance forced them to move fast.

"The noise is getting to me." Marko tried to talk over the artillery blasts. He was too tired to chew the hard bread.

"The shells or the screaming men?" Karl drank some tea.

"Both." Marko shivered, thinking of the man with the shot-off arm. Remarkably, the medic thought he might survive.

Niilo nodded. "Folks like to pretend soldiers die quick in battle. Just one bullet and down. But it ain't like that."

Marko looked at his whiteovers, which were smeared with dirt and blood. "Isn't the shelling ever going to stop?"

"Might not be good news if it did," Niilo said.

"Why?" Marko yelled over an explosion.

"They usually shell the other ridge," Niilo said. "This might mean they're trying to soften us up for an attack."

"If only we had artillery to fire back," Marko said.

"Our boys on the other ridge have a handful of mortars," Niilo said, "but they're useless without a field telephone to direct fire. And their few old cannons are so low on ammo that they're saving them for an emergency."

"This isn't an emergency?" Marko asked.

"Not even close."

It shook Marko to think what a real emergency might be.

CHAPTER 18

FIRE IN THE SKY

The shelling continued for two days. At night the muzzle blasts of the Russian regimental guns lit the sky with red fire, and by day the haze from the explosions blocked the sun.

Except for brief naps and food breaks, Marko and Karl stayed on duty the whole time. They hauled water, blankets, and supplies to the hospital tent. They helped pull injured soldiers up the hill, and they carried food to the trenches.

In the middle of the second night the barrage finally stopped, and Marko fell into a deep, dreamless sleep.

The sky was still black when he woke to a sound he'd never heard before. Time froze as a steady *chunk puff, chunk puff, chunk puff* rose from the valley.

Marko sat up. "What's that?"

Karl said, "The Russkies are starting their tanks."

Marko pulled on his boots as the sound of the engines quickened. A great beast was awakening in the dark and breathing faster and faster.

Kerola lit the kerosene lamp, and Marko tasted sulfur in the back of his mouth as the wick flared. He looked at his watch. Four in the morning.

The lieutenant nodded at Juho and Seppo. "You saw this one coming, boys. Thanks to your report we've got our positions reinforced."

Then he turned to Marko and Karl. "Are my messengers ready for a night ski?"

"To HQ?" Karl asked.

"Yes." The lieutenant gave a packet to Karl. "You boys will be delivering this one. I need Niilo here."

Marko tried to look alert, but his brain was numb from lack of sleep and the constant pounding of the shells. As he stepped outside, the crunch of the snow under his boots told him it was well below zero. Luckily, a half moon made it easy to see.

Without a word, Karl put on his skis and started down the trail. Marko followed, finding the woods much darker than the moonlit hillside.

Marko had never heard a tank attack, but there was no mistaking the sound in the valley when the engines revved to a higher pitch and started forward. The metal-on-metal grinding of the gear cases sounded like a giant circular saw ripping through the woods.

A Russian flare burst against the night, and green

light filled the sky. The boys stopped and stared at the battlefield. Marko felt a chill up his spine as the white-washed tanks trundled toward Horseshoe Hill. Blue flames shot from the back of the engines as the drivers accelerated up each bump and then slowed at the top, their headlights bouncing wildly.

The Russian infantry marched ghostlike behind the tanks. Just when Marko thought the noise couldn't get any louder the battle cry rose up: *"Urra! Urra!"*

The full assault was on.

But no Finnish troops were in sight. *Why aren't we fighting back?*

"Hurry!" Karl planted his poles and pushed forward. As Marko followed, the barrel of a tank cannon flashed, and a shell exploded at the base of Horseshoe Hill. Orange flames leapt from the tanks; explosions rocked the ridge. Still no Finns fired back.

The boys skied hard, ducking under branches and squinting in the shadows. Behind them the cannon fire was now mixed with the pop of hand grenades and the staccato spit of machine guns. Tanks ground forward, but the only answer from the Finnish side was a rifle shot and a short burst from a Suomi submachine gun.

"Aren't they ever going to fight back?" Marko asked.

Just then a Finnish machine gun opened up from Horseshoe Hill. Bullets rang off tank armor. The Russians returned fire. Then a charge exploded with an echoing *whomp.* Marko looked over his shoulder and saw flames.

"We got a tank!" Karl yelled.

Karl stopped suddenly, and Marko nearly skied into him.

A face washed by moonlight stared at them. "Ahhh . . ." Marko sucked in his breath to hush his scream. The body of a Finnish soldier hung from a tree. His jacket was gone, and a note tied to his suspenders read: *Accept your liberation!* The fingernails had been ripped off his left hand.

Marko coughed and gagged. He was shaking so badly that he dropped his left ski pole. Were the Russians crouched in the woods, waiting for them? A metal taste burned his tongue as he peered into the shadows and bent to pick up his pole.

"They're hoping to scare us." Karl tried to sound brave, but his voice cracked.

The boys skied forward as quietly as they could, scanning both sides of the trail. Marko cringed each time his ski bindings or his brace creaked.

When they reached Company One, Karl told their lieutenant about the dead soldier.

"You didn't touch the body, did you?" he asked.

"No sir." The boys shook their heads.

"Good. Last week those Russkies booby-trapped a corpse. I'll send a couple of men with you to retrieve the body."

Marko was relieved to have the soldiers ski partway back with them. But as soon as he and Karl were alone, Marko whispered, "We should have asked to borrow a rifle."

"Too late now." Karl's voice trembled.

Marko led the way back, skiing fast in the open
stretches and slowing down on the corners in case a
Russian squad was approaching. Despite the battle
noise in the distance, the squeak of the boys' skis jarred
Marko's nerves. If the Russians caught them, would
they shoot quickly, or dangle them from a tree branch
first?

After pushing hard up a hill, Marko slowed as he
approached a bend in the trail.

"Almost there," Karl whispered.

"Good," Marko said.

Suddenly something jumped across the trail at
Marko's feet, and he almost squealed. A rabbit dashed
for the woods, its rear legs kicking up snow.

Marko took half a stride forward and froze. Over the
blasts from the battlefield, he heard a scraping sound.
Someone was coming. "Find cover!"

He slipped off his skis and scanned the forest.
Getting out of the moonlight and into the shadows was
their only hope. "Cover your tracks," Marko said, picking up his skis and poles and stepping off the trail.
Taking the biggest strides he could, he tried not to drag
his boots in the snow. Karl followed close behind. After
they'd taken only half a dozen steps, the other skier
sounded as if he was about to come into view.

Marko set down his skis and knelt in the snow. Karl
dropped beside him. As Marko threw his white hood
over his head, he glimpsed the tall hat of a Russian soldier as the man came skiing over the hill, moving stiffly.
The last thing Marko saw before he ducked his head

and lay down was the red tips on the collar of the Russian's greatcoat. Marko held his breath and prayed that their whiteovers would hide them.

Wet snow stuck to Marko's face mask, and his heart pounded as the squeak of the Russian's skis got louder. Machine guns rattled in the distance. Would the soldiers hear Marko's heart beating from the trail? He imagined one of the Russians aiming a rifle at his head.

The soldiers skied closer. Marko prayed they wouldn't stop. Snow melted down the back of his neck and his cheeks turned numb, but he lay perfectly still. Though the cramped muscles in his leg shot needles up to his chin, Marko clenched his teeth. He could feel Karl shaking beside him.

The skiers slowed down, and a man grunted something. Marko was about to make a dash for the trees when the Russians started up again. Marko heard Karl take a deep breath.

Marko waited a long time before he whispered, "You think it's safe?"

Karl lifted his head. "They must be out of hearing by now."

"Think there's a second patrol?"

Karl got up and peered down the trail. "Looks clear," he whispered, and brushed the snow from his clothes. "That was a close call. I can still smell their rotten tobacco."

When Marko tried to stand up, his weak leg turned under him, and he fell back into the snow.

"What's wrong?" Karl asked.

Marko rubbed his calf. "I'll work it out."

"Thanks for keeping quiet," Karl said. "We were this close to being strung up like that other fellow." Karl held his fingers a centimeter apart. Then he helped Marko to his feet.

"We did good," Marko said.

The boys reached the command trench at dawn. The Finns had beaten back the advance, and the hillside was eerily quiet.

Niilo pointed to Hoot Hauta. "You're looking at a hero, boys. A tank was about to crush one of his men when he ran out and dragged the fellow clear. Then he ducked behind the tank and set it on fire with a Molotov cocktail."

Hoot shrugged. "I did my job like any man would." He nodded at Marko and Karl. "Glad to see you boys are back."

"I'll second that." Juhola took the packet from Karl.

"We saw a Russian patrol," Karl said.

"I never would have sent you out if I'd known how far the Russians were going to wander," the lieutenant said. "But the good news is you're safe. I'll wager that patrol never saw you."

"We hid in the snow," Marko said.

"Good work! I've got another mission for you."

"Another message?" Marko asked. He was so tired that he didn't think he could ski another kilometer.

"No," the lieutenant said. "I'd like you to collect some war booty. We sighted two Russian horses bolting past the field kitchen. The trail should be easy to follow in this snow."

Karl suddenly pointed. "Look at that!"

Marko turned. The sun was rising over the battle-field. Beyond the trenches a charred tank with its turret still smoldering was tipped on its side in an antitank trap. The whitewash had peeled off the tank's armor in places, showing patches of green paint, and the worn steel tracks sparkled in the morning light.

Then Marko saw where Karl was pointing. Frozen in place like a toy soldier, a dead Russian leaned against the side of the tank with his eyes fixed straight ahead. His black fur cap and his eyebrows were coated with white frost. A pistol clenched in his right hand pointed toward the ground.

Marko gulped and stared. "I didn't believe Joki when he said men could freeze that fast."

The lieutenant said, "The crew jumped out and ran, but that fellow chose to fight."

Fallen Russians lay everywhere. Many looked like young schoolboys. Some were sprawled flat in the snow, but others had a knee or an arm pointing sky-ward. Rifles, spiked bayonets, caps, helmets, and am-munition boxes littered the ground. Near the tank a pile of Russians had fallen on top of each other. Marko could see bloody bullet holes in their greatcoats. Only last night these frost-covered heaps had been men eating their supper and writing letters home.

"You're not going to believe this!" Joki yelled. He had climbed out of the forward trench and stuck his head into the engine compartment of the tank. "My English ain't so good, but I think this here nameplate says 'Liberty.'"

Marko and Karl ran down to look at the ten-ton monster. The tank smelled of burnt paint and gasoline. Inside the hatch were rows of unfired brass shells. Marko peered into the cramped interior and saw a car-type steering wheel and foot pedals along with piles of empty machine-gun magazines.

Marko walked to the rear and looked over Joki's shoulder. The markings on the big V-12 engine read *Liberty Moth XII*. Marko turned to Juhola, who had followed them. "Is that Liberty as in America?"

"It's an American aircraft engine."

"So the whole time we've been hoping for aid from the United States they've been selling equipment to Russia!"

The lieutenant nodded. "Cicero once said, 'Money forms the sinews of war.' " He stared at the smoking battlefield for a long time.

Finally he turned to Marko and Karl. "You boys better get after those horses while the tracks are still fresh."

CHAPTER 19

WAR BOOTY

As the boys skied across the hillside after the horses, Marko fumed, "I can't believe those Americans are selling tank engines to the Russians!"

"See, you can't depend on nobody but yourself," Karl said.

"I'm sweating bad—time for Niilo's trick." Marko pulled out a fresh undershirt and stripped to the waist. "Don't you believe it helps?"

"Don't you ever mind your own business?"

While Marko buttoned his coat, Karl pointed to some hoofprints. "Here they are."

Marko looked down. "The spacing shows they're moving fast."

"They must really be spooked."

The trail crossed an open field and then mean-
dered through a logged-over area where the horses
had stopped to nibble aspen saplings. "They're eating
bark," Marko said. He thought of Tuuli back home in the
barn.

"At least they're walking now," Karl said.

Finally the boys spotted the horses, standing at the
edge of a cedar swamp. Their bridles dragged in the
snow as they munched on branch tips. "Take it slow,"
Karl said as he slipped off his skis.

"They're huge compared to Finnish horses!" Marko
said.

When Karl stepped toward the shaggy animals, the
largest horse planted his feet and faced them with his
nostrils flared.

"That big bay is the leader." Karl kept his voice low.
"If we get him on our side, it will be easy to corral the
other one."

The bay horse's ears were straight up, and his tail
switched from side to side. He looked ready to bolt.
Then Karl said, *"Idi syuda, mal'chik."*

To Marko's surprise the horse nickered softly.

"What did you say?" Marko whispered.

"My mother taught me a little Russian. She used to
say that when she called our gelding. It means 'Come
here, boy.' "

Then Karl pulled a carrot from his pocket and re-
peated, *"Idi syuda, mal'chik."* The horse moved toward
them.

"Where'd you get that?" Marko asked.

"From the cook. In case the lieutenant wanted me to take care of Kahvi," Karl said.

"So that's why Kahvi likes you so much," Marko said.

When the bay reached for the carrot, Marko caught his bridle. The horse jerked back, but Karl said, *"Spokojno, mal'chik,"* and patted his shoulder.

"Let me guess," Marko said. "That means, 'Easy, boy'?"

"You pick up Russian fast," Karl laughed.

Marko was relieved to see Karl smile. "If we lead him, the other should follow," Marko said. Indeed, as soon as they started down the trail, the second horse fell in line behind the bay.

"How did you learn to handle horses so well?" Marko asked.

"We owned a pretty chestnut named Salla."

"We had a pair of chestnuts named Tuuli and Teppo. But they drafted Teppo into the army."

"They let us keep Salla because she was our only horse."

"We should think of a name for these horses," Marko said.

"How about Joseph and Cheslav? After Stalin and Molotov. Molotov's first name is Vyacheslav."

"That's a good one," Marko said.

Karl grinned.

"How long have you been in the Junior Civil Guard?" Marko asked.

Karl's mood suddenly changed. "None of your business."

After skiing all night, Marko had lost his patience. "I didn't know there was a law against making conversation."

Karl looked ready to snap back. But he turned to Marko instead. "Can you keep a secret?"

"Sure." Marko nodded.

"We're friends, aren't we?" Karl looked at Marko.

"I'd like to have a friend."

"I came here because I had nowhere else to go." Karl paused as if he couldn't decide whether to continue or not. "I'm not in the Civil Guard."

"Really?"

Karl nodded.

"Wow! Where did you get the uniform?"

"It belonged to my brother."

"I promise not to tell," Marko said.

"There's more." Karl took a deep breath. "The morning the war began I was in the barn feeding the cows. My brother would have been with me, but he stayed in the kitchen to talk over his wedding plans with our parents. I was about to start the milking when I heard screams from the house." Karl's voice quavered as though he was about to cry. "Then there were rifle shots."

Karl stopped, and Joseph nosed his shoulder. Karl patted the horse's neck.

"I ran to the barn door and looked out. Two soldiers spotted me. I ducked back inside, but they chased after me and cornered me in a stall. When the first man saw how young I was, he laughed and leaned his rifle against the wall. Then he pulled out a knife."

Karl's eyes welled up with tears, and his shoulders sagged. "The one with the knife lunged toward me. He was so close. . . ." Karl closed his eyes. "I'll never forget the stink of tobacco on his breath . . . the cold stare . . . that blade flashing at my throat. I reached back and grabbed a shovel. I swung it as hard as I could. The next thing I knew, his head was split open. He fell backward. Blood splattered everywhere. It was awful, Marko." Karl lowered his head and cried quietly. "Then—"

"You don't have to say anything more." Marko shuddered. *How terrible it must feel to kill someone.*

"No, I want to tell you everything." Karl wiped his eyes with his mittens. "Then the second soldier made a move for the rifle, but I grabbed it first and he ran.

"When I got to the house I found my mother and sister lying in the kitchen. Their dresses were torn and . . ." Karl's voice got so quiet it was hard to hear. "I could tell they'd fought hard. My father and brother were dead, too.

"I was about to get sick to my stomach when I heard shouts. I looked out the window and saw more Russians coming. I grabbed my skis and my brother's Civil Guard rucksack, sneaked out the back door, and headed into the woods."

"You put on his uniform?" Marko asked.

Karl nodded. "Once I got clear of the Russians." Then he went on, "I skied south. The next day Juho and Seppo found me. I told the lieutenant I wanted to fight on the front lines, but he said he'd only let me stay if I agreed to be a messenger."

"Does he know the whole story?" Marko asked.

"Just that my parents are dead. You said you wouldn't—"

"I won't tell anyone," Marko said. Now he truly understood Karl's bitterness. Marko knew how lucky he was to still have his family, even though they were scattered across Finland and Sweden. He prayed that everyone was safe.

"There's one more thing—" Karl stopped.

"What is it?"

"Nothing. We'd better get these horses back."

It was midday when they returned to camp. The lieutenant smiled as he inspected the horses. "Mission accomplished!" he said. "These are fine mounts. They look hungry, but we'll get them back in shape."

"Karl named them Joseph and Cheslav," Marko said.

"After our archenemies," Juhola chuckled.

Kerola stepped forward and picked up the reins of the bay. "Should I bring the horses to the stable, sir?"

"Good idea. You both deserve a reward. How about if we take you off double spark duty?"

"I could use some extra sleep," Karl said.

"Me too." Marko grinned.

The big bay suddenly snorted. Marko looked up as the horse reared and jerked the bridle out of Kerola's hand.

"Stop," Kerola yelled as both horses ran up the hill. Marko expected the animals to break for the woods;

instead they wheeled and trotted back to Karl. The lieutenant laughed as the bay sniffed Karl's pocket, looking for another carrot. "Looks like you've made yourself a friend. You and Marko better turn Joseph and Cheslav over to the teamsters yourselves."

"Will do," Karl said.

CHAPTER 20

LETTERS HOME

Marko woke to the sound of hushed voices. He was still wearing his coat and boots and lying on top of his blanket. It was dark outside, and the lieutenant was talking to Juho and Seppo. "Don't take any unnecessary chances, but the more intelligence you gather, the better for us all."

"We know a few tricks," Juho said.

Marko was surprised that Juho and Seppo left with only a light pack and a pistol between them.

Marko sat up and rubbed his eyes.

"Awake already, Koski?" the lieutenant asked.

"Why didn't they take their rifles?"

"They're going on a different sort of mission tonight."

When Karl woke, Kerola gave the boys an order.

"Now that the shelling has stopped, you two help clear the forward trenches before that dirt freezes."

"Let them have their supper first," Juhola said. Then he turned to Marko and Karl. "And if the action heats up down there, scoot back to the command trench at the first whistle of an artillery shell."

During supper Karl frowned. "I'm getting sick of this watery stew every night. At home we cooked up a *liha-soppa* soup that was loaded with meat, potatoes, carrots, and onions."

"My mother made that, too," Marko said.

"But my favorite meal was our *silakkalaatikko* casserole," Karl said. "I get hungry just thinking about it. . . . Marko?"

"Yes?"

"Thanks for listening this morning. I needed to talk . . . but I didn't know who to trust."

"I know what it's like to hold something inside," Marko said. "My friend Johan was the only person I could talk to."

"Is he in the Civil Guard, too?"

"Not anymore," Marko said. He told Karl the story, and he was grateful for the darkness that hid his tears.

"That must have been awful," Karl said.

"It felt like . . . having my chest crushed . . . I don't know. . . ." Marko sighed. "We better get going." He knelt and washed his mess kit in the snow.

"There's something else I should tell you," Karl said.

"What is it?" Marko started down the hill.

"Can you keep it a secret?" Karl walked beside him.

"What could be a bigger secret than you not being in the Civil Guard?" Marko said.

"This would be really hard not to tell, and it would ruin everything if it got out."

"I know how to be a friend," Marko said.

"You're sure?"

Marko nodded, but Karl still hesitated.

"Well?" Marko asked.

Karl looked back up the hill. "You won't tell?"

"I said I wouldn't."

Karl glanced over his shoulder and whispered, "I'm a girl."

"What!" Marko stumbled and almost fell. "You're a—"

"Quiet!" Karl said. "I wanted to fight the Russians, but I was sure they wouldn't let me join if they knew I was a girl."

"You've got to be kidding. I—"

"Keep your voice down," Karl said.

"Karl Kangas is a girl," Marko said, as if he was trying to convince himself it was true.

"I knew this was a mistake. Would you quiet down!"

"What's your real name?" Marko lowered his voice.

"I can't tell you. You might let it slip out."

"I said you could trust me," Marko said.

"Call me Karl. And hush, there's the trench up ahead."

*　　*　　*

The whole time Marko and Karl helped the infantry squad clear their trench and realign the log rifle rests, Marko could think of nothing but Karl's secret. As Marko breathed in the scents of burnt powder and damp earth, and as he watched the steam rise from the infantrymen's shoulders, one thought was stuck in his mind: *Karl Kangas is a girl.*

While Marko was in shock, Karl seemed relieved at having shared his secret.

Marko tossed a shovelful of dirt onto the outer berm, and Karl said, "Doesn't it feel strange to be digging in dirt with snow all around us? The smell reminds me of planting time."

"My mother says the same thing when she steps into our root cellar. Most women are happy to card wool and knit and sew in the winter, but she gets lonesome for digging in her garden."

"She sounds like a special lady."

"She loves the outdoors. And she's a crack shot with a .22 rifle." Marko bent to scoop up more earth, sighing. "I thought we were done with shoveling when we finished the horse shelter."

"The dirt work never ends around here," Karl said. "There's always a fresh hole to be dug or an old one to be cleaned out. It was the same way back on our farm. By the time I finished weeding the last row of potatoes, I had to start all over again at the top of the field."

After Marko and Karl had dug their way to the far end of the trench, Marko asked, "If I guess your name, will you tell me if I get it right?"

"Stop it, Marko."

"But I can't be thinking of you as Karl when you're a girl. Is it Aliisa?" he asked.

"Marko!"

"Or Anna? If you won't give me any hints, I'll just go through the alphabet until I get it."

"I've got to be Karl to you and everyone else, or you'll ruin everything. You've got to think of me as a boy. Quiet now. Someone's coming."

When they were still shoveling after midnight, Karl said, "I almost wish the Russians would fire a shell so we could go up to the command trench and rest."

"I feel like I could sleep standing up," Marko said.

"Your leg must be killing you. I don't know how you keep going."

"I'm used to it," Marko said, rubbing his calf. "My mother taught me to break every job into small steps. When I'm digging I take it one shovelful at a time. When I'm skiing I never think any farther ahead than getting to the top of the next hill. But right now my back aches a whole lot worse than my leg."

Karl's shovel made a *ting* as it struck metal, and he knelt down and brushed away the dirt.

"What is it?" Marko asked.

"A Finnish helmet." Karl lifted it in the silvery moonlight.

"Look at the bullet hole." Marko pointed at a neat dot above the front brim. The back of the helmet was ripped open.

Marko watched as Karl knocked the dirt out of the

helmet and turned it over. When Karl saw the crusted black blood inside he turned pale.

An infantryman took the helmet from Karl and called to one of his friends. He looked at the stained insides. "Ain't it awful what a machine gun can do to a fellow?"

Another soldier bent down and said, "This must be his, too." He pulled a worn leather mitt out of the dirt. It had big holes in the fingers. "No wonder he complained about the cold."

"What should we do with it?" the first man asked.

"It's no good to us," the other said. They tossed the mitt and the helmet over the berm and into no-man's-land.

Marko and Karl got back to the tent just after dawn. As they took off their coats, Marko reminded himself: *Don't give away Karl's secret.*

A voice called, "Special delivery," and Juho and Seppo stepped inside.

Juho opened his pack and dumped a pile of letters and papers onto a blanket. His uniform and his hands were stained with dirt and dried blood.

"Those Russkie uniforms was froze like boards." Seppo squinted as he took off his steamed-up glasses and wiped them on his sleeve. "We had to slice open their pockets with our knives. Found some extras, too." He showed a tobacco pouch, a badge with a red flag painted on it, and a pin with a hammer and sickle.

"Keep that Russian tobacco clear of me," Niilo said. "It stinks like burning garbage."

Karl spat out, "I hate that smell."

Marko stared at the table. He couldn't believe the lieutenant had sent Juho and Seppo out to search dead bodies.

Juhola saw Marko's eyes. "It's an ugly business," he said. "But if we can gather intelligence that saves our men, we have no choice." He turned to Juho and Seppo. "Find anything unusual?"

"Just regular stuff," Juho said. "The Russkies haven't run out of black bread yet."

"I can see that." The lieutenant knelt and picked up a wrinkled envelope. The flap had been sealed with a half-chewed glob of black bread. He opened the letter and handed it to Kerola, who read slowly as he translated from the Russian.

My dearest wife,

Nothing has changed. Finland is cold, dark, and miserable. I don't know why we would ever want to invade such a country. They promised us that the Finns would lay down their guns and receive us with open arms. We are not being greeted with flowers and parades. If the politruks weren't guarding our rear, we would all turn and go home.

"*Politruks?*" Juho asked. "Them political officers?"

"Yes," Juhola said. "They watch the rear lines. Any man who shows a hint of cowardice is shot."

Kerola scanned the rest of the letter. "He goes on to

complain more about our desolate country and sends his love to his kids."

Marko thought of the soldier's family waiting for his return. How many weeks or months would it be before they found out he was dead?

And how is Father? Dear God, please keep him safe.

"This one is from an officer," Kerola said, opening an envelope with a bloodstain on the corner. He read silently for a minute. "It's to his brother-in-law."

> *I would give up everything—my commission, my property, and all my rubles—to escape this place. We have sent tanks and infantry against the Finns with no success. They hide in the woods and in trenches so we can never get a clear shot. We have no idea how large their force is. One day we sent 150 men to attack. Only 23 returned. That leaves us no choice but to sit and wait for—*

"*Belaya smert,*" Juhola finished, looking over Kerola's shoulder. "I know that one. It means 'white death.' "

Kerola nodded. " 'That leaves us no choice but to sit and wait for white death to come.' "

"Save that one," the lieutenant said. "We'll send the letters with useful intelligence to HQ. Put on your reading glasses, Mr. Kerola, they brought you a pile of homework."

Marko stared at the letters. The reality of war was so different from the bright August day when he and

Johan had received their Junior Civil Guard certificates.
A band had played, and the boys had marched in shorts
and new military caps. Then each of them had shaken
the local lieutenant's hand. At the end of the ceremony
they'd saluted the flag and recited a poem called
"Soldier Boy":

> *The field of glory was his world,*
> *He always stood merry and steady*
> *Where he had taken his place*
> *In fire, in blood . . .*

A field of glory? Marko shook his head. *All I've seen
out here on the front is fire and blood.*

CHAPTER 21

CHRISTMAS ON THE FRONT

On Christmas Eve afternoon Marko and Karl stopped by the stable to visit with the Russian horses. Joseph nickered and perked up his ears the minute he saw Karl.

"Joseph sure likes when you talk Russian to him," Marko said.

"I don't think it matters what I say." The horse pushed his nose into Karl's hand. "He's just lonesome for home."

Joseph sniffed all of Karl's pockets for a treat. Then he suddenly raised his nose and pushed Karl's cap off, knocking a hidden carrot to the ground. "You can't fool him," Marko laughed as Joseph picked the carrot up and munched it.

When Joseph had finished his snack, he laid his neck across Karl's shoulder so Karl would pet him.

"I've seen horses lean against my father when he's

shoeing them," Marko said, "but I've never seen one do that."

"I'm lucky he doesn't put his full weight on me."

"He'd flatten you like a bug," Marko laughed.

As Marko and Karl were walking back toward the tent, Kekko let out a yell. "We're gonna have us a Christmas feast!"

Juho and Seppo had skied into camp pulling a sled loaded with a sack of flour and a pickle barrel.

Juho nodded. "We found an abandoned store behind the Russian lines. It was empty except for this stuff in the cellar."

The cooks didn't have milk or baking powder, but they whipped up a batch of pancakes, with fat garlic pickles for dessert.

Kekko was the first to sample the pancakes. He doffed his crooked helmet to the cooks. "After this little war is done, you boys should think about opening a pancake restaurant."

Marko tasted one of the flat-looking pancakes and frowned. "A little sugar would have helped," he whispered to Karl.

"They're chewy," Karl said, "but these are mighty fine pickles." He took a crunchy bite and grinned.

The front was dark and quiet on Christmas Day. Snow clouds kept the sky gray, and the Russians showed no sign of moving. The men were given limited duty for a change, and Marko used the extra time to rest and write to Mother.

Marko and Karl were the first ones to get back to the tent after lunch. Marko pulled out his *puukko* knife to open a letter from home. Karl was sitting next to him. Marko leaned forward and whispered, "Is your name Elsa, by chance?"

Karl ignored him. Marko said, "Or how about—"

"Didn't you listen to a word I said?" Karl kept his voice low. "When I first got to the front, all I wanted to do was die. I can't tell you how many times I thought about skiing toward the Russian lines and letting them shoot me. Why did I deserve to go on living when my whole family was dead? But the longer I've been here, the more I realize that my purpose is to be a part of this fight. And for that to work I've got to be a boy."

"I felt the same way after Johan died," Marko said.

"You understand, then?" Karl touched his hand.

Marko nodded. Karl would have to stay a "he" in his mind.

When Niilo lifted the tent flap, Karl jerked back his hand and asked Marko, "Is that knife handmade?"

"It's my father's design." Marko showed Karl the carved handle as Niilo and the rest of the men walked in. "We made it in our shop. From the time I was little I'd sit at the kitchen table and draw outlines for blades and handles."

Niilo walked over. Had he seen Karl touch Marko's hand? But Niilo pulled out his own knife and said, "Take a gander at this."

"A reindeer antler handle," Marko said, turning the edge to the light, "and a well-honed blade."

"I made it myself," Niilo said.

"Very nice," Marko said. He handed it back and used his own knife to open the letter.

"Good news?" Karl asked.

"You want to hear it?"

"Sure."

Dear Marko,

I hope that you are warm and safe tonight. I'm trying not to worry myself sick over you and Father both being in harm's way. I still haven't heard from him.

Whenever I see a sleigh approaching the hospital, I pray you aren't lying in the back. But at the same time, the sleigh drivers are a blessing since they bring me your letters.

It's been an agony to have my family gone, but I keep telling myself that Finland's freedom is worth our sacrifice. Christmas is only a few days away, but holiday spirit is in short supply. The blackout applies to Christmas lights, of course, and candles are not permitted in the cemeteries. But even if we can't light a candle for Grandpa, we can all say a prayer for him.

And you can be sure I will be praying for you and all of the brave soldiers.

Marko smiled when he read about the candles. "My family used to have so much fun at Grandma's on Christmas," Marko said. "We got up early when the sky was still black and walked along the riverbank to church. As we got closer, we saw candles glowing in the windows. The heat melted away an arch in the middle of each frosty pane, giving the snow a golden—"

"Does little Marko miss his mommy?" Seppo looked over Marko's shoulder.

"Why don't you mind your own business for once?" Karl said.

"Our messenger boys have joined the same crybaby club."

Juho and the rest of the men laughed.

The lieutenant looked at Marko and Karl. "Do you have your skis waxed?"

"They're ready to go," Marko said.

"Tomorrow HQ is sending over a fellow to help our signals man lay a phone line. You'll lend him a hand."

The next morning Marko was looking forward to the change in routine until he saw the huge coils of wire piled on the sleigh.

"That looks like enough wire to go all the way to Helsinki," he said.

"Just to HQ," the signals man said.

Marko and Karl helped the men load the wire onto smaller sleds and pull them through the woods. Marko's hands were soon numb from wrestling the wire around rocks and through the brush.

Marko told Karl about the time he and Johan had collected barbed wire. "At least we don't have to worry about phone wire cutting our hands."

Karl said, "And there's another good thing about this job."

"What's that?"

"The farther we go, the lighter our load gets."

The following afternoon the signals man made the final connection to the command trench and handed the lieutenant his field telephone. The lieutenant smiled. "Not only will this save you messengers some trips," he said, "but if the Russians start a big push, we'll be able to call in mortar support."

Later, when Marko and Karl headed back to the tent, Marko said, "The phone reminded me . . . of that morning in the church tower with Johan. I can't get over how normal that day was. We were talking and joking. Then we heard the bomber engines . . ."

"It was the same for me when the soldiers came to our farm," Karl said. "One minute I had a milk pail in my hand, and the next thing . . ."

"I can't imagine . . . and then to have them come after you . . ."

Karl nodded. "I didn't want to run."

"But you had no choice," Marko said.

"I've tried to tell myself that." Karl hugged himself as if he was cold. "But it doesn't stop the nightmares."

CHAPTER 22

BELAYA SMERT

On New Year's Day Karl and Marko were returning from delivering a message to HQ. The lieutenant used the telephone when he could, but the connection was often broken, and important dispatches still needed hand delivery.

"I never dreamed I'd be celebrating New Year's this way." Karl's breath steamed out of his face mask, and his eyelashes were covered with frost. An icicle hung from his chin.

"Me neither," Marko said. His skis squeaked to a stop when he stopped poling. He took off his mitts and pressed the backs of his hands against his eyes to melt the ice.

"That's better," Marko said, flicking the water from

his eyes. Then he shoved his hands under his coat to warm them.

Karl did the same. "It's got to be colder than thirty-five below. My lips are so numb that I feel like I'm mumbling."

"The metal on my brace feels cold enough to break."

"If I had to ski with that thing strapped on my leg, I'd give up on the first hill."

"I just tell myself how easy skiing is compared to what it was like learning to walk again." Marko put his mitts back on and flapped his elbows to warm up his arms.

"Didn't you feel like giving up?"

"Every day. But with my family cheering me on—especially Mother—I couldn't let them down."

Karl's head dropped.

"I'm sorry I mentioned my family," Marko said.

"That's all right," Karl said. "We'd better get going." He planted his poles and kicked forward with a squeak of his skis.

They got back to camp after dark. It was so cold that the smoke was trailing flat off the stovepipe above the tent and then sinking toward the ground.

Hoot Hauta, who often went outside without a coat, was wearing a hat and mitts and talking with the lieutenant. "These temperatures strain the equipment," Hoot said. "The rifles and the Suomi submachine guns jam unless the infantrymen dilute their gun oil with kerosene."

Juhola said, "And when the fellows get careless and touch bare metal, it rips their skin right off. The medics are treating more men for frostbite than gunshot wounds."

Spark duty for Marko that night meant twice the usual number of trips to the woodpile. And it was so cold inside the tent. His feet stayed warm because they pointed toward the stove, but his stocking-capped head was freezing. "Look at this," he whispered to Karl as he got ready to take his turn watching the stove. He blew out a puff of air and watched it turn to frost.

Outside, a sniper's rifle popped in the dark. "You can tell how cold it is by that sound," Karl said.

Marko nodded. Instead of a sharp report the rifle made a flat crack. "It sounds like somebody wrapped a blanket around the barrel."

Along with the cold front, a blizzard blew in from the north, and it snowed for days. The deep drifts in camp kept the boys shoveling all day long to keep the paths open.

After watching Juhola go through his daily ritual of shaving on a twenty-five-below-zero morning, Marko asked Karl, "Why does he go to all the trouble?"

Karl picked up a snow shovel. "You think the lieutenant should go around with a soot-blackened face and a beard like everyone else?"

"Even Kerola is growing a beard," Marko said.

"By shaving every day the lieutenant shows that he appreciates order and cleanliness," Karl said. "Most of these men stink worse than barnyard animals."

"You just say that because you're a gir—"

"Shut up!" Karl looked back toward the tent.

"So you think the lieutenant keeps neat to remind himself of the order we left behind?" Marko asked.

"Exactly," Karl replied. "It's his way of saying something against the craziness of this war."

"Unlike certain demo men," Marko said with a smile.

Karl laughed.

To help the men deal with the cold, the lieutenant changed the duty schedule to balance periods of action with rest. So that a messenger was always available, Marko and Karl alternated shifts with Niilo. Each day followed the same pattern:

Two hours patrol
Two hours rest
Two hours action
Four hours sleep
Sauna every third day

The sauna time was welcomed by the men. And Marko helped Karl sneak into the sauna after the men had gone to bed. Karl tried to be quick, and Marko guarded the door.

"I know how much my little sister likes to wash up and look nice," Marko said.

One night when Seppo and Juho were returning from a sniper mission, they caught Marko standing by the sauna. "You lost, mechanical boy?" Seppo's voice shot out of the dark.

"I . . . thought I heard something"—Marko spoke extra loudly to warn Karl—"and I came up here to look."

"Whereabouts?" Seppo blinked. He'd been skiing hard and his glasses were steamed up.

"Up there." Marko pointed toward the woods.

"That's where we came from, dunce," Juho said. "You just heard our skis."

The two of them headed toward the tent.

The men celebrated the first sunny day of 1940 with a sauna. Marko was grateful for the chance to steam away the lice, which had now spread to every man in camp. Though Marko burned his long underwear every time Mother sent him a new pair, he found there was no escaping the itchy bites of the pests.

"With all our scratching and our runny noses we look like a bunch of sick monkeys." Joki coughed as he took off his underwear bottoms and shook them out.

Once the men were seated on the sauna benches, Kekko asked the lieutenant, "How about another Paavo Nurmi story?"

"Remember what I told you about Paavo and the '24 Paris Olympics?" Juhola asked. The men nodded.

"The thing that impressed me most wasn't Paavo's back-to-back wins in the fifteen hundred and the five thousand. And it wasn't his win later that week in a cross-country race on a day so hot that twenty-four men collapsed before they reached the finish line. The thing that showed me the most toughness happened the evening after the fifteen-hundred-meter race. That night our team took a bus from the Olympic village in Colombes to Paris, which is ten kilometers. On the way to town we looked out the window, and there was Paavo walking all the way to Paris!"

Marko smiled. If Paavo Nurmi could walk ten kilometers after winning two gold medals, he shouldn't complain about a little skiing and snow shoveling.

Later Hoot asked, "Are we ready for a roll in the snow? Whenever I sit here soaking up hot steam, I can't help but think of those Russkies shivering by their campfires."

Kekko said, "We heard they're so short on food they're eating their horses."

"Don't tell me you're feeling sorry for them Red devils," Seppo said. His eyes looked even meaner with his glasses off.

The lieutenant said, "Most of that regiment are green recruits, young boys from south Russia. That's why they wear those lightweight uniforms."

Hoot nodded. "And you gotta remember they're everyday fellows like you and me. None of them asked to be sent here."

"I just hope they keep stoking up their bonfires," Seppo said. "It makes them mighty sweet targets."

Marko understood Hoot's feelings. What would it be like to be camped in a strange country in the middle of the winter, knowing the very fires that kept you warm made you a target for white-suited snipers who stalked the forest and brought *belaya smert*?

CHAPTER 23

THE FIELD TELEPHONE

During the second week in January the weather warmed to above zero. And more good news came from the northern front.

"They're hitting the Red Army hard up on the Raate road." Kerola looked up from his newspaper. "Our counteroffensive wiped out Russia's Forty-fourth Division!"

As the men cheered, Karl gave Marko a thumbs-up.

Marko read the rest of the front page. Ten thousand Swedish homes had volunteered to take in Finnish refugees. In her letters Mother said that Grandma and the children were doing fine, but Marko still worried about them. If only another country would send troops to Finland and help end the war!

"How can the whole world sit back and watch us fight alone?" Marko asked.

"Only Sweden has the guts to step forward," Kekko told him. "They're sending troops."

Hoot said, "I hear Norway will help."

"I'm still counting on America," Marko said.

"Those folks are famous for speeches but short on deeds," Joki said.

The warmer weather brought another snowstorm. When the snow eased, the lieutenant met with his platoon leaders in the tent. "If any of us was in charge on the other side, we all know what we'd do."

Hoot nodded. "This could be their chance to try a break."

"We can't let them rejoin their main unit."

Two mornings later the sky was black and still. Marko was dreaming of Christmas rice pudding. He'd just scooped out an almond—a sign that the year ahead would be filled with good fortune—when he woke to what sounded like a huge thunderstorm.

Marko and Karl jumped into their clothes and ran to the command trench. The red muzzle flashes of the Russian regimental guns lit the sky. The shells screamed in with a high-pitched whistling and plowed into the hillside. Dirt clods and hunks of blasted roots and rocks flew everywhere.

The Finnish troops hunkered down and waited.

At dawn the Russian tanks drove out of the woods

and lined up in attack formation, but their artillery support kept firing. "It's odd they haven't stopped shelling," the lieutenant said.

Thick clouds of dust and exhaust made it hard to see. Marko couldn't stop coughing as the tanks crawled toward Horseshoe Hill with the sound of steel grinding on steel.

"They're coming right at us." Karl's eyes were wide.

As the sound of the tanks got louder, Marko's heart beat so fast that he felt light-headed.

Karl looked sideways at him. "You all right?"

"I just realized I was holding my breath," Marko said.

"Me too."

"Every squad's in place, sir." Kerola's voice was so shaky that Marko could barely hear him over the artillery.

The lieutenant handed his field glasses to Kerola. "What do you think of that?"

"They're veering north." Kerola sounded confused.

"And running for the road."

"That can't be," Kerola said. "We've got the road blocked with felled trees."

"They plan on making their own trail," the lieutenant said.

Marko squinted into the smoky haze. Instead of attacking in a broad formation the way they usually did, the tanks were in a single column and heading northeast just out of rifle range. A squad of infantrymen on snowshoes packed the trail ahead of the lead tank. Every few minutes they traded off with rested men.

"If the tanks get over that rise, they'll be no stopping them." The lieutenant turned to Kerola. "Send two platoons and the antitank squad to head them off." Then he spoke to Niilo. "Report back once the men are in position, and I'll call in mortar support."

As Kerola and Niilo ran out of the trench, Juhola picked up the phone and cranked the handle. "It's dead!" He swore. "Company One is standing by to direct mortar fire for us."

He cranked the phone again. Nothing. "Where is that signals man? He went out at dawn to check the line."

Marko looked at the dead phone and felt a chill. He thought back to the first day of the war. "We'll go," he said.

"What?" the lieutenant asked.

"We'll check the line," Marko said.

"No," Juhola said. "I promised your mother—"

"You need everyone else to defend the hill," Marko said. "Karl and I can look out for each other."

"Right!" Karl said.

The lieutenant studied the approaching tank column. Finnish snipers had dropped a few of the snowshoers, but other men had taken their places. The cannon fire kept the Finns pinned down.

"Very well." He handed a small roll of wire and some tape to Marko. "All you'll need is this and your knife." He took off his holster and pistol and handed it to Karl. "Just in case."

Staying low, Marko and Karl ran out of the exit trench, put on their skis, and started down the trail.

Marko kept an eye on the wire, and at the same time he watched for Russian soldiers, though he knew one pistol wouldn't help if they met an enemy patrol. There was a good chance that the Russians who'd cut the line would be waiting to ambush the repair crew.

As Marko skied down the second ridge and rounded a corner, he stopped. The twisted body of the signals man lay beside the trail. He whispered to Karl, "Do you know how to use that pistol?"

"I've only shot a rifle," Karl said, pulling the gun from the holster and handing it to Marko.

Marko set his poles down and skied forward slowly, keeping the pistol ready and eyeing the forest on both sides. Just before he reached the fallen man, he saw a movement to his left. Karl gasped when Marko turned and aimed at the woods. Marko was about to squeeze the trigger when a Siberian jay flashed its orange belly and flew from a tree.

"Whoa!" Karl said.

Marko tried to steady himself as he looked at the bulging eyes of the fallen signals man. The fellow had been shot through the chest, and a section of wire had been tied around his neck.

Marko avoided the man's face as he dropped to one knee and went to work fixing the line. The whole time Marko shaved the insulation from the broken wires, he imagined a Russian sniper aiming at the back of his head. His hands shook so much that he slipped and cut his thumb. After Marko had twisted the wires together, Karl wrapped a turn of tape around each splice.

Marko and Karl were only halfway back to Horseshoe Hill when a mortar fired. The phone was working! Company One was blasting away. By the time they reached the command trench, Niilo was reporting to the lieutenant, "Those rounds slowed the Russkies enough for our boys to pepper them good."

Juhola turned to Marko and Karl. "Excellent, excellent work, gentlemen."

Niilo clapped both boys on the back. "You'll have to tell us the whole story."

Machine guns fired to the north, followed by an explosion. "That sounds sweeter than Sibelius," Juhola said.

Sibelius' name reminded Marko of the music he and Johan had found in the old hermit's shack. *How strange to think of that now.* Marko took off his mitt to check his cut thumb.

The lieutenant smiled. "Now that you've been wounded in action we'll have to put you in for a medal."

CHAPTER 24

A FROZEN HELL

On the sixteenth of January the temperature dropped to the coldest so far—forty-seven below zero.

But the weather didn't slow down the Finns, who stuck to the lieutenant's plan of mixing periods of rest with rapid action. After naps in their tents, they used small groups of skiers to mount night raids against the Russians. The quick attack-and-retreat tactics kept the Red Army off balance.

One afternoon Kerola said, "There's more good news in the newspaper. The novelist Selma Lagerlöf donated her Swedish Academy medal and her Nobel Prize to a Finnish aid group."

Somebody hollered, "Mail call!" outside the tent. But it was only Kekko. He walked up to Marko. "When I saw this package with your name, I thought I'd do a good deed and bring it over."

"How nice of you," Marko said.

Kekko smiled. "What sort of treats do you think Mother sent us this time?"

"Us?" Marko pulled out the letter but ignored the package.

"I was thinking you might be willing to share with a buddy who was kind enough to lug this heavy parcel over here. Need some help with that string?"

Mother had sent two loaves of rye bread and a dozen apples.

"Apples! A fine treat on a winter's day," Kekko said.

"And I'll bet an apple and fresh bread is even better." Marko sawed off a piece of rye and handed it to Kekko.

Before he tasted an apple, Karl said, "Suppose we could share one with our Russian friends?"

Marko smiled. "Joseph and Cheslav would love that."

"Don't waste 'em on horses!" Kekko's mouth was full.

"It won't hurt to split one between them," Marko said.

Karl looked at the letter. "Any word on Jari and Nina?"

On January 17 the temperature hit fifty-six below zero.

That afternoon Kerola put Marko and Karl to work splitting firewood. "At least it's not windy," Karl said, pounding his mitts together to warm his hands as he handed Marko the axe.

"If there was a wind, I'd risk a court-martial by telling Kerola to split his own wood." Marko's voice was muffled by his woolen face mask, and his eyelashes were crusted with ice.

When Karl laughed, his breath froze on his scarf. "At least we don't have to ski today."

"We wouldn't glide at all." Marko scrunched his boot down to test the snow. "I keep thinking how I used to complain about the heat in our forge. Standing by those coals—"

"Would feel so good right now!" Karl said.

"It shouldn't be this cold with St. Henry's Day only two days off," Marko said. St. Henry's Day celebrated the life of a bishop who was martyred on a midwinter mission to Finland.

Karl nodded. "My father used to tell us to stand behind the barn on St. Henry's Day and listen hard. If we heard a bear roll over in his den, that meant winter was half over."

"On the evening of St. Henry's Day the kids in Virtalinna used to race down the street shaking bells and banging sticks on houses to break the back of winter," Marko said. "Johan had a drum that he'd pound on as we ran."

"It's going to take more than a stick to break this cold."

As Marko hefted the axe, Karl said, "Let's pretend every block of wood is the back of winter—give it a good crack."

When Marko returned to the tent, he needed to put salve on his sore leg. Marko hadn't let Juho or Seppo see his brace since the first day, but the cold hurt so much that he didn't care.

Neither man said anything as Marko unbuckled his brace. For a moment he thought they were going to leave him alone. But when he reached for the homemade salve Mother had sent him for Christmas, Seppo said, "Does our mechanical man need oiling?"

"Baby oil," Juho said.

Marko slid his long underwear up and rubbed on the salve. The odor of pine tar and honey filled the tent.

Seppo blinked and sniffed. "Perfume."

Karl said, "If that's too sweet for you, why don't you go suck on one of those smelly foot rags?" He pointed at the clothesline above the stove.

Marko grinned. That was the sort of thing that Johan would have said.

"Listen, pup . . ." Juho stepped toward Karl, but the lieutenant bent down and picked up Marko's jar.

"Homemade?" he asked.

Marko nodded. "The secret ingredient is honey."

"Can I use some on my shoulder?"

The next day the Russians staged a surprise attack. Three tanks sped toward the Finnish trenches with infantrymen running behind.

"More scrap iron heading our way," Hoot Hauta said

as he left the command trench to check the position of his squad.

"Why didn't they shell us first?" Kerola asked.

The lieutenant said, "Their artillery must be frozen up."

The tanks started firing their cannons and machine guns from long range, but the Finns held their fire.

The tanks roared across a frozen ditch, bumping up and down and spinning their tracks wildly. The Russian infantrymen in their brown greatcoats gave out a brave *"Urra!"* as they struggled to charge through the deep snow.

When the enemy had almost reached the Finnish trenches, Hoot ran toward the first tank, followed by Joki and the scarecrow outline of Kekko.

Hoot lifted up a log and was about to shove it into the tank treads when something exploded beside him. The whole squad dove into the snow.

The other squad members jumped up, but Hoot lay still. Kekko ducked behind the tank and threw a Molotov cocktail onto the rear deck. Flames shot out, and the tank veered left and stopped. The hatch flew open, and black smoke poured out as soldiers leapt to the ground, their backs and legs on fire. Machine guns greeted them.

Marko held his breath and stared at the place where Hoot had fallen. Suddenly Hoot wobbled to his feet. But instead of dodging his way back to the trenches, he swayed like a drunk.

Kekko was running toward Hoot when the Russian

infantry opened up. Bullets ripped into Hoot's uniform.
"No!" Karl shouted. Hoot's body jerked violently as
more bullets hit.

Marko closed his eyes as Hoot fell into the snow.

The medics couldn't reach Hoot until after the
Russians fell back. It was dark by then. Their faces were
grim as they pulled the sled past the command trench.

The lieutenant asked, "Is he bad?"

A medic said, "He took three bullets."

Hoot's eyes were closed, his face covered with frost.
His hands were so cold they had turned blue—blue like
the dead boy Marko had seen on his way to the front
that first day. *Not Hoot.*

After the medics started up the hill, Karl took off his
mitt and wiped the tears from his eyes.

As soon as Karl and Marko finished their duty, they
ran to check on Hoot.

"How is he?" Marko asked the head medic as they
rushed in.

"I'm sorry," the medic said. He pointed to a table in
the corner where a body lay, draped by a sheet.

"I can't believe it," Karl said.

"Of all the men . . . why him?" Marko fought back
his tears.

The medic said, "I never would have picked him to
go down, either. And he was our only casualty today."

A man from the soup cannon walked in with a coffeepot. "Would you fellows care for a cup of coffee?"

Before anyone could answer, a voice behind Marko said, "Coffee."

Marko and Karl turned. Hoot's big hand reached out from under the sheet and pulled it off his face. Karl squealed and jumped backward. Marko's heart stopped.

"My Lord!" The medic walked over to Hoot. "Do you know you've got three holes in your chest?"

"I was pretty numb. A grenade knocked me flat."

Marko was amazed at how easily Hoot talked.

"You didn't have a pulse when they brought you in here!" The medic opened Hoot's shirt. "I was about to send you to the cooling tent. You must have been all frozen up. The wounds have started to bleed now."

"Am I leaking?" Hoot asked.

"Just a little. You can thank the cold for saving you from bleeding to death."

"I like winter," Hoot said. "Better patch these holes or . . ." His head dropped back.

"Bring me my sewing kit," the medic told his assistant.

Marko and Karl stared. "Will he be all right?" Marko asked.

The medic touched Hoot's wrist. "His pulse is strong. His color looks good. He just might pull through."

"I knew he was too tough to die!" Karl said.

"It'll take more than a few bullets to do Hoot in." Marko punched Karl's shoulder.

CHAPTER 25

THE NAKED TRUTH

"Ain't it nice not to have to shovel down our spuds before they freeze to our mess kits?" Niilo said. It was the first week in February, and the sunlight was increasing every day. Today the temperature had warmed to twelve below zero.

"Feels like summer." Seppo stretched. The men were on the east side of Horseshoe Hill, looking out over a snow-covered field as they ate their lunch.

"I wonder where Joki and Kekko are," Karl said.

"Kekko's always first in line at mealtime," Marko said.

"Wiring a few more booby traps on the road," Juho told them.

Niilo turned. "Ain't that Joki and Kekko right there?"

Marko looked down the ridge. Two men were skiing hard toward them.

"I've never seen them move that fast." Juho stood up.

"Why don't they have whiteovers on?" Seppo asked.

"Whiteovers nothing." Juho stared. "Those boys is plumb naked."

Everyone burst out laughing, except for Karl, who looked down at his food.

Marko couldn't believe his eyes as he watched Joki and Kekko race up the hill. They were wearing nothing but their boots and dog tags. Kekko's hair was standing straight up, and his dog tags were bouncing off his skinny white chest. Both men were red-faced and puffing and looked as if their knees were about to buckle. Marko laughed so hard that he almost choked on a piece of hardtack.

"Those two will try anything for a laugh," Niilo said.

Then Marko noticed that Karl wasn't the only one not laughing. The lieutenant had stepped to one side and was peering past the skiers. He turned to Juho. "I don't like the look—"

A bullet whizzed over Juho's head and smacked into a tree.

"Your rifle, Juho!" the lieutenant said, pulling out his pistol and running to the edge of the woods.

Juho and Seppo grabbed their rifles and followed. More bullets clipped bark off the tree above Marko's head.

The lieutenant yelled, "Down!" to the skiers, as Juho

and Seppo leveled their rifles. Joki and Kekko both dropped.

Another shot cracked below.

Juho and Seppo fired several quick rounds. Then it was quiet. Juho looked up from his sights. "I think we got 'em."

"Good work," the lieutenant said. Then he turned to Kerola. "Organize a patrol and see what's going on out there. If those snipers were forward observers, we've got to find out how big their main force is."

Meanwhile, Joki and Kekko got back on their feet and skied up the slope. Marko was shocked at the sight of them. They were flushed from their sprint, and branches had cut their faces and arms. Kekko had a piece of a cedar bough tangled in his left bootlace, and Joki's shoulder was bleeding.

"Just what is going on?" the lieutenant said.

"We got caught," Joki said.

"Doing what?"

"Taking a sauna," Joki said.

"A sauna!" the lieutenant exclaimed.

"We're real sorry, Lieutenant," Kekko said. Instead of making an odd face the way he usually did, he looked stunned.

"It was a big mistake," Joki admitted. "After we finished setting those trip wires, we ran across an old sauna."

"You started a fire in broad daylight?" the lieutenant said.

"We hadn't seen hide nor hair of the Russkies for so

long, we figured it wouldn't hurt none," Joki said. "We'd just heated her up when bullets started flying. We stepped out to look. Our clothes was inside. We never thought—"

"Thinking is something that you utterly failed to do." The lieutenant was angrier than Marko had ever seen him.

"We didn't mean no harm," Kekko said.

"Go clean up," the lieutenant said. Then he turned to Kerola. "We'd better contact HQ." Marko and Karl followed the officers down to the command trench.

When the lieutenant hung up the phone, his lips were tight. He turned to Kerola. "HQ just got a confirmation. A fully armored Russian regiment is coming from the east to relieve the forces that we've had trapped in the valley. Let's hope those snipers didn't get back to them with our coordinates."

Marko felt his stomach tighten.

"What are our alternatives, sir?" Kerola couldn't hide the quavering in his voice.

"I suggested that we ski out in a wide circle tonight and use another *motti* maneuver to split the Russian force and surround them, but the major doesn't want us to risk an advance strike. He's afraid we might get trapped between the regiments."

"So we retreat?" Kerola sounded relieved.

"I don't like that word. But he ordered us to pull back to the main ridge immediately. We'd better get started. The more time we have to shore up our defenses, the better chance we'll have of standing firm."

The next four days were frantic. Working day and night, the soldiers hauled supplies and equipment, re-erected the tents, set up a field kitchen, moved the horses, and built a stable.

Both of the Russian horses did their part pulling loaded sleds. Joseph always nickered when he saw Karl and nuzzled his hand, expecting a carrot or a pat. Sometimes the big horse laid his neck over Karl's shoulder and rested it there, staring into the distance as though he was dreaming about a warm barn back home.

"That animal's a workhorse," Joki scolded. "Don't be coddling him like some lapdog!"

The worst job of all was digging new trenches in the frozen ground. Since Seppo and Juho were out spying on the approaching Russian regiment, Joki and Kekko were assigned to help Marko and Karl with the command trench.

As Kekko scraped away the snow, he said, "A fellow working on a foxhole yesterday told me the frost is about a meter deep."

Karl swung a pick to test the dirt, and it bounced off the frozen ground with a clink. "It's like cement."

"We'll have to use a few muscles, then," Kekko said. But his pick barely dented the ground.

Through the morning the men tried picks, iron bars, and bayonets to chop through the frost.

During lunch, Marko looked at the blisters on his

hands and said, "I can't decide which hurts worse, my hands or my leg."

Karl slipped off his mitts. "I've got blisters on my blisters."

When the lieutenant walked by, Kekko said, "We been thinking that this hard ground could do with a little extra persuading. If I was to take a small charge of dynamite and—"

"What good would it do to blast out a trench if we let the Russians know exactly where to aim their shells?"

"But we—" Kekko said.

"Think less and dig more," the lieutenant said.

"I have an idea," Marko said.

"What is it, Koski?"

"Since the Russians can't see smoke at night, why don't we build a fire to thaw the ground, like they do in the cemetery?" Marko recalled the frozen dirt piled beside Johan's grave.

"Good idea. After dark you and your partners get to work."

One night of hot coals thawed the ground enough to allow the men to break through the frost by the middle of the next morning. When they finished the trench, Joki said, "I gotta hand it to you, messenger boy, using them coals was good thinking."

"Marko's a good partner," Karl said.

Marko did the math. *We'll be facing four thousand Red Army soldiers! The odds will be ten to one against us!*

Everyone was silent.

Then Kekko spoke up. "We got us a big problem."

The men turned. If Kekko was worried, they were in trouble.

"I can't see any way around this one." Kekko shook his head. "I don't know where we're gonna find room to bury all those Russkies."

Everyone burst out laughing.

"Take your positions, boys," the lieutenant said.

Joki was grim. "Now we toast Comrade Molotov."

The Russian tanks began grinding forward as the first pink light filtered through the pine tops. Their infantry marched close behind. The huffing of the engines lifted a blue cloud of smoke, while the vibration of the gear cases shook the ground.

But as loud as the tanks were, Marko's blood ran cold when the Russians' shout, *"Urra! Urra!"*, drowned out the clattering engines. The branches of the pines trembled as if a great wind was blowing out of the east.

Hoot raised his arm. "Go get 'em, boys."

Marko watched the lead tank power forward. Despite the stream of Finnish machine-gun fire, the tank kept coming. His ears rang as red tracer bullets ricocheted off the armor and arced into the sky. The tank rammed a

CHAPTER 26

RED SHOES, OR SHEEP TO THE SLAUGHTER

At dawn Marko looked down on the valley from the new command trench. The Russians had stopped their artillery barrage, and the largest force of soldiers that Marko had ever seen was lining up behind the Red Army tanks. The regiment now wore whiteovers like the Finns.

Marko didn't need field glasses to know that the three Finnish companies dug into the hillside were in for the fight of their lives.

Hoot Hauta studied the battlefield, too. Instead of going to the hospital he'd stayed on to help plan their defense. "They got two regiments after us now."

"More like a regiment and a half," the lieutenant said, "if you figure their losses before reinforcements arrived."

thick birch tree and brought it crashing down over a trench. But when the tank tried to cross the trench, it slipped a track and got hung up. The tank gunner fired bursts as his two crewmen jumped out with a jack and a crowbar. But Finnish machine guns cut them down.

One wave of Russians after another charged the Finnish trenches. The machine gunners mowed them down, but more men kept coming, hurdling the bodies of their fallen comrades.

"How can they keep rushing?" Karl said. "It's suicide." Unlike the first morning on the trail, when Karl had looked on the dead enemy soldiers with glee, his eyes looked sick today.

"Russians fight with courage but without imagination," the lieutenant said. "They're taught to charge straight forward." Marko could barely hear him over the cannon fire. "Stalin kills off any general who has a mind of his own, leaving him with nothing but sheep to send to slaughter."

Just then a man ducked into the end of their trench. *A Russian!* Marko leapt up.

No. An ammunition bearer for a machine gunner.

"We're running low on ammo," the man reported to Juhola. "Two men are down. And we've melted one barrel." His face was flecked with dirt and sweat.

"Messengers," Juhola said, "help him lug some fresh ammo belts."

The next thing Marko knew, he and Karl were standing beside the ammunition supply wagon with a metal box of machine-gun belts in each hand.

"This way." The ammunition bearer ran into the woods. He was carrying a box of his own along with a replacement barrel and a can of coolant. Marko and Karl hustled as the man scampered down the hill.

The machine-gun emplacement was tucked between two spruce trees overlooking the battlefield, but the smoke made it hard to see. Two tanks burned below. Instead of short pops and bursts as in the other battles, the gunfire was a constant roar.

"Coolant! Good," the gunner's assistant shouted. "That steam was drawing cannon fire." Thousands of empty brass cartridges lay at his feet.

"Thanks, boys," the squad leader said to Marko and Karl. "Hand me a belt." The gunner's assistant pushed it into the gun from the right side, while the gunner pulled the leading edge through and levered the first shell into the chamber.

As Marko and Karl ran back up the hill, the Maxim machine gun added its rounds to the already deafening noise.

When the Russian attackers fell back late in the afternoon, the lieutenant said, "That's round one."

In the momentary quiet Marko heard something strange. "Is someone singing?"

"Your ears are ringing," Kerola said.

"That *is* a song," Niilo said.

The men in the command trench watched as a Finnish soldier shuffled up the hill toward them. He was singing softly and clutching something in his hands.

Then Hoot, who was closest to the man, said, "His guts, poor fellow." The soldier's stomach had been torn open, and he was cradling his intestines in his hands.

As a medic ran to tend to the man, Marko knelt at the end of the trench and threw up.

Marko heard the man shout, "No. Leave me alone. I promised her I'd be home before dark."

Then he pitched forward into the snow.

An hour later, Kekko and Joki led five Russian prisoners up the hill. The Russians were quiet except for a short man who babbled and waved his arms. As he passed the command trench, Karl said, "I don't think that little guy is a soldier."

"You can't believe those Russkies," Kerola said.

"Karl—you know Russian?" the lieutenant asked.

"A few words. He says he's a fisherman from Kemi. He was shopping for his wife last week. He bought her red shoes. On the way home soldiers grabbed him and made him enlist."

Juhola chuckled. "That's a great story."

"He says he still has the shoes in his pack," Karl said.

"Don't believe him," Kerola warned.

The lieutenant waved to Kekko. "Bring that fellow over here. Let's see what he's carrying."

When Kekko pulled a pair of red ladies' shoes out of the man's pack, the men all laughed. And Marko laughed the loudest of all, as the relief at surviving the battle washed over him.

"He must like high heels," Joki said.

"Not quite his size," the lieutenant said.

Kekko held one shoe next to the Russian's boot. It was ridiculously small. "He may be telling the truth," the lieutenant said. Then he turned to Kerola. "Ask him his name."

The moment the man heard Russian, he beamed. "Petya." He pointed to himself. "Petya Filipovii."

"Let's call him Poppi," Hoot Hauta said.

Juhola nodded. "Show Poppi to our soup cannon."

"No cannon!" Poppi spoke with a heavy accent.

The men laughed again.

"We're going to feed you, not shoot you," the lieutenant said.

CHAPTER 27

THE LINE WILL HOLD

"War is a messy business," Juhola said as he glassed the enemy formations from the command trench. "I hate how every answer is the wrong one. Kill, kill, kill. If the mothers and fathers could see what happens to their boys out here, there would never be another war."

It was the third morning of the Russian offensive, and he was talking to no one in particular. He set down his field glasses but kept staring toward the east. "They line them up. We mow them down. To want this butchery— Stalin has no soul! Aurelius said the best way to seek revenge is to not become like the wrongdoer, but Stalin will be taking a good number of us to the devil with him before this is done."

*   *   *

For the next two weeks, despite a cold wave that swept down from the arctic and the snowstorms that followed, the Russians attacked again and again. They isolated one company with a full assault. Then they stormed all three at once.

"Our line must hold!" the lieutenant said.

Marko knew that if one Russian unit broke through, they would be helpless to defend the rear, and Virtalinna would fall. The Finnish machine gunners and the anti-tank squads kept the Russians at bay, but the one thing they couldn't stop was the artillery.

Marko had a constant headache from the guns pounding them day after day. Some of the older fellows gave up on sleep altogether and stayed up playing cards or whittling. Marko always fell asleep, but he woke whenever the guns stopped.

One night when Marko and Karl lay down for their sleep shift, Karl said, "I can't believe they haven't run out of shells. I'm going to be deaf by the time this war is over."

"They say the men defending at Kollaa have taken a month of shelling. They're still holding on."

"I'd go crazy," Karl said.

"Would you squirrels shut your yaps so a man can sleep?" Juho hollered.

The artillery didn't injure many men, because the Finnish positions were so well camouflaged. But the explosions caved in part of the trenches every day. When Marko and Karl weren't shoveling snow or running messages or helping the medics, they spent their nights helping the infantrymen dig.

The toughest thing to handle, other than a man be- **177** ing wounded, was a horse getting shot. Late one afternoon a horse bolted into no-man's-land and went down in the cross fire.

Marko thought the horse was dead. But as soon as the Russians fell back, it started bawling. Every few minutes it lifted its head and gave out a strangled cry.

No one in the command trench spoke, but Marko could see the tension in the men's faces every time the horse bawled. Karl looked ready to cry.

Finally, Niilo said, "I'll go," and he grabbed a pistol.

But before he reached the exit trench, the lieutenant said, "Someone's already taking care of it."

A Finnish soldier had climbed out of a forward trench and was walking toward the wounded horse. Instead of ducking down, as Marko expected, the man kept his head high.

When no one fired from the Russian side, Niilo said, "I'll be switched. Them Russkies have hearts after all."

The battlefield was quiet when the soldier stopped over the horse. The last time the animal lifted his head he didn't bawl.

The pistol fired once, and an awful silence descended.

The soldier walked back toward the Finnish trenches with his eyes cast down. He was only a few paces from his trench when a machine gun barked from the Russian side. The bullets tore into his back and spun him around.

Karl gasped as though someone had punched him.

"Those damned pigs," Juho said between clenched teeth.

The man fell to his knees, and a second burst chopped him down.

When the temperature dropped to forty-three below zero the next day, the lieutenant said, "Our old friend Winter is back."

The dry, bitter cold of January had been hard on Marko's leg, but the damp cold of February made it hurt even more. When Marko and Karl put on their skis to make a run to HQ, Marko couldn't stop shivering. "This weather might be a friend to the lieutenant," Marko said as he fumbled with his binding strap, "but I wish they could reschedule this war for summer."

Karl laughed.

Despite the cold and the constant bombardments, Marko was amazed at the high morale of the Finnish army.

"We're teaching those Russkies it ain't so easy to move a Finn once he gets his feet planted," Kekko said.

"Maybe if they upped the odds to twenty to one against us, they'd stand a chance," Niilo said.

One of the main reasons for the men's good humor was the new sauna. Though Hoot wasn't strong enough to chop logs, he'd supervised the construction. And he made sure that it was fired up every third day.

Hoot was fond of saying, "Sauna cures all ills."

The Russian captive, Poppi, also helped keep spirits

high. He turned out to be a friendly mascot to their company. Over the protests of Kerola, the lieutenant let Poppi help Marko and Karl chop firewood and shovel snow. In the evening he sang and danced for the men. And everyone laughed at his Finnish. All he could say was "yes," "no," "big cannon," "capitalist dog," and "put up your arms and surrender."

Karl and Marko took Poppi to the stable to show him the two Russian horses. On the way up the hill Poppi said something to Karl, and the two of them laughed.

"What's so funny?" Marko asked.

"I only understood part of what he said, but as close as I can figure, his commander told him that we Finns tortured our prisoners, and he's happy that we are nice boys."

"Tell him he's nice, too," Marko laughed. "It's hard to think of a man as your enemy when you can look into his eyes."

When they reached the stable, Marko expected Joseph to nicker for Poppi and perk up his ears the way he did for Karl, but the horse barely noticed his new visitor, even when Poppi chattered in Russian.

"It's not just the Russian talk," Marko said to Karl as they walked back to the tent. "That horse really does like you."

The men were also cheered by the news that the famous Finnish runners Paavo Nurmi and Taisto Mäki were visiting America to promote the Finnish war effort. They'd even been invited to the White House.

But the Finns had a big problem: lack of ammunition. Supplies of every caliber were getting dangerously low.

"Pretty soon we'll be left fighting with bayonets and vodka bottles," Kekko said.

February passed without news of American aid, but the men still didn't give up hope. One night in the sauna, Hoot said, "I figure the longer we hold out, the greater the chance the Brits or Americans will join up with us."

"Or the Frenchies," Kekko said. "If they're smart, they'll want to be on the winning side."

Kerola wasn't so positive. "According to the papers," he said, "the U.S. Congress keeps debating whether they should send aid, but they've allowed U.S. companies to sell millions of dollars' worth of munitions to Russia."

"I've got a cousin in Duluth who's trying to enlist in the Finnish army," Hoot said. "If it was up to him, America would send soldiers tomorrow."

"Too bad your cousin isn't named Roosevelt," Marko said.

CHAPTER 28

A WATERY GRAVE

"Wake up! Everyone up!" the lieutenant said.

Marko rolled over and rubbed his eyes.

"Just got a call. The Russian infantry is set for a big push at Company One. The major needs our support so that the Russians can't outflank him to the north."

Just then Juho and Seppo returned from their patrol. "The Russkies are up to mischief again," Juho said, breathing hard.

"We heard," the lieutenant said. "Lining up to hit Company One."

Seppo shook his head. "That's a decoy. Since dark they've been moving equipment through the woods toward the lake."

"The land north of Company One is all swamp," Marko said.

Juhola turned to him. "Are you sure?"

"An army could never march through there. My friend and I bog-walked it last summer." Marko stopped. Had he spoken too quickly? But the lieutenant's mind was made up.

"Very well. I wonder why it's taken the Russians this long to think of trying the lake. You and Karl scoot down and tell Kerola that we'll be putting our Keskijarvi defense plan into place. I want a meeting of my platoon leaders in five minutes."

When Marko and Karl delivered the message, Kerola said, "HQ's not going to like this."

By the time Marko and Karl got back to the tent, Juhola was showing Hoot a hand-drawn map of the lake. "There's only one shore low enough for the Russians to land their equipment. That means they'll have to cross this bay." He made an X. "If we set the charges along here"—he drew an arc—"we should be able to block any advance."

He turned to Marko and Karl. "How are your chopping muscles?"

"Firewood tonight?" Karl asked.

"Your ice-chopping muscles."

"We're going to mine the lake!" Marko said.

For the rest of the night every soldier in the company who wasn't in the trenches helped the demo team plant explosives under the ice. "This is my kind of ice fishing!" Kekko exclaimed, grinning as he lowered a charge into a hole.

To mask the sound of the chopping, Joki knocked the muffler off a Russian tractor that had been captured by the Finnish infantry, and he set the engine at a fast idle beside the lake.

While the demo men placed the charges, the lieutenant ordered the artillery battery to wheel two cannons into position above the lake and camouflage them with spruce boughs. The cannons, recently donated by France, had the year 1877 stamped on their barrels and looked so old that Marko wondered if they could fire.

"Are we going to use those guns if the charges don't work?" Marko asked Hoot.

"Not if," Hoot said. "*When* the charges work."

But Hoot looked worried. Was the plan too complicated? Marko couldn't understand why the lieutenant would want to blow the Russians up and then shell them, too. What if Marko had been wrong about that swamp? If the Russians pushed to the north instead of coming this way, the line would collapse, and with it Finland's hopes.

Late in the afternoon on the following day the Red Army targeted Company One with an all-out assault. The lieutenant immediately got a call from HQ. "Yes," the lieutenant said into the phone, "I'm certain."

He looked at Kerola after he hung up. "Napoleon

said the first rule of warfare is to never do what the enemy wants you to. But if I'm wrong about this attack, I'll be busted down to peeling potatoes."

The command group skied to an observation point above the lake. "No sign of movement yet," Hoot said. The cannon fire of the tanks attacking Company One echoed in the distance.

The woolen masks of the Finnish soldiers dispersed their frosty breath as they waited. Every man knew that if the Red Army's northern attack wasn't a decoy, all three companies were doomed.

Marko thought: *I hope Mother doesn't know how close the Russians are to breaking through the Finnish lines.*

The lieutenant scanned the far shore with his binoculars. "Nothing."

The men listened to the battle raging in the north.

At midnight the lake was still quiet. Karl whispered, "You suppose the Russians moved their equipment to trick the lieutenant?"

"If he's wrong, we're in deep—" Marko stopped. "There's your answer." A faint rumbling rose from the far shore. Karl and Marko punched each other's arms.

One by one the engines cranked to life, and the Russian tanks started across the lake, raising plumes of snow and blue exhaust in the moonlight. The infantry marched close behind, with horse-drawn sleighs bringing up the rear.

When the Russians neared the section of the lake

that had been mined, Juhola turned to the artillery observer at his side. "Ready your guns."

The artillery battery pulled the boughs from their cannons. Karl looked at the guns' wooden-spoked wheels. "I hope those old things don't blow us up when they try to shoot them. We have one just like it in our village museum."

One artilleryman patted a rusty cannon. "Time for Hyppy Heikki to say hello to the Russians."

"Why would he call a gun Jumping Henry?" Marko asked Karl.

"No idea," Karl said.

The Russians continued to advance. "Haven't they reached the charges yet?" Marko asked Niilo.

"Cross your fingers. We got to time it right," Niilo said.

When the tanks were three-quarters of the way up the bay, the lieutenant said, "Now!"

Hoot waved to his demo men. Explosions shot columns of water high into the air. As the ice heaved upward, Marko felt the ground shake under his feet.

Three tanks fell through the crack in the ice, and the others skidded forward as the ice began breaking under them. Even with their tracks reversed, the tanks kept slipping toward the black water. Soldiers climbed out of the hatches and tried to leap onto the ice. Some slid into the water. Others went under clinging to the turrets.

The horses pulling the sleighs reared at the noise. When a few tanks managed to turn around, the horses' panic grew. Marko saw Karl's face tense up as several animals fell.

Yells went up from the Russians as they retreated, and the sharp cracks of rifle shots soon echoed from behind their lines.

"*Politruks.*" Niilo shook his head. "Killing their own men!"

The lieutenant shouted to the artillery observer: "Fire at will."

The muzzle blast of the first cannon nearly knocked Marko down. The flash lit up the whole ridge, and the spruce trees on both sides shivered and swayed, knocking clumps of snow to the ground. The recoil sent the gun carriage flying backward five meters before the hitch plowed into the ground and stopped. The second gun kicked back with the same violence.

"Now I see why it's called Jumping Henry," Karl shouted as the gun crew hustled to roll their cannon back into position.

The shells whistled over the Russian soldiers and exploded chunks of ice and water by the far shore.

"Missed by half a kilometer!"

"Right where they were aiming," Hoot said as the gunners unleashed a second volley.

When a big hole opened up at the rear of the Russian formation, Marko realized that the lieutenant intended to trap the Red Army between two open leads. Rock cliffs blocked any escape to the north and south. That left the soldiers facing a watery grave.

The cannon volleys continued as men screamed and

fell through the ice. Marko imagined the burning chill of the water. A few soldiers struggled back to the far shore, but as they broke for the woods, the Finns had set up a Maxim machine gun to finish the job the *politruk*s had started.

"What a horrible way to die," Karl whispered.

Marko nodded, staring down the lake. Of all the killing that Marko had seen, this was the most brutal. The Russians could run and face the hot rain of machine-gun bullets spitting from the woods, or they could stand their ground and slip into the black water.

CHAPTER 29
CEASE-FIRE

One week after the lake battle, the men were standing at the edge of the woods finishing breakfast. Kerola ran up the hill and handed the lieutenant a paper. "It's official!"

Juhola read: "March thirteenth. Russia and Finland signed a truce agreement in Moscow at one o'clock this morning. The war will end at eleven o'clock."

The men all cheered.

"And nobody thought we could hold the line!" Joki said.

"We taught those Russkies a lesson they won't never forget," Kekko said.

"Hope we captured Leningrad," Joki shouted, "so I can spend a night in that palace! Put my boots on the czar's pillow!"

"There's more," Kerola said.

The lieutenant shook his head. "Hear the terms of the peace agreement before you celebrate. If this information is correct, Finland has agreed to cede thirty-five thousand square kilometers. The Karelian Isthmus and areas north of Lake Ladoga, including Sortavala, Käkisalmi, and Virtalinna, will be incorporated into the Soviet Union."

"Not Virtalinna!" Marko said. "Never! Never!"

"The Russkies attacked *us*," Kekko said. "Why should they get anything?"

"War doesn't determine who's right," Juhola said, "only who's left standing. The important thing is that we held the front. Stalin thought this was going to be a walk in the park, but we showed him that Finland isn't about to give up. Hold your heads high! Finland is still independent!"

Everyone looked down and shook their heads. Soldiers who had joked in the darkest moments of the war were silent. Kekko stared into his bowl of half-eaten porridge. Juho and Seppo walked off toward the woods.

Marko stood in shock. Karl pulled on his arm. "Come on."

When they got back to the tent, Marko said, "I can't believe it! We held the line but lost the war? After all the bloody battles, the dead, the skiing, the frozen hands . . . and now Virtalinna's gone."

"It's not fair!" Tears ran down Karl's cheeks. "No! First I'm left an orphan, and now this. It's just not fair."

"Karl . . . I'm sure things will work out for you,"

Marko said. Yes, his own worries were small compared to Karl's. A farm could be replaced and a forge rebuilt, but what if his whole family had been taken from him?

A short while later, the lieutenant entered the tent and asked Marko and Karl, "Ready for one last trip?"

"Where to?" Marko asked.

"No need for a packet this time. HQ called and said a squad from a neighboring company is bivouacked east of the lake. Those men don't know this little tea party is about to end, and we're afraid they might engage the enemy. Pity for someone to die on the last morning of the war. I told HQ I'd send someone to warn the squad."

"Easy skiing on the snow crust," Karl said.

"I'll see you after the war is over," the lieutenant said.

Marko and Karl started down the trail. The sky was blue and the air still. Compared to the dark days of December, the sun was so bright that Marko had to squint. He paused on a birch hillside where a flock of redpolls was testing their spring voices. He poked the hard-packed snow with his ski pole. "We won't have to worry about following the trail. Johan and I used to love exploring new territory on a day like this."

Marko led the way down the slope, skirting the shore of the lake and passing the place where the Russian infantry had retreated. The twisted arms and legs of soldiers stuck up out of the snow. A drift covered a stalled tank up to the top of its treads. Ravens and foxes had been feasting on a pair of horses that lay tangled in the traces of their sleigh.

Marko stopped. Just ahead someone had uncovered several Russian soldiers and stripped them of their medals.

"The lieutenant will be upset if he finds out," Marko said.

"It scares me, Marko." Karl's voice was only a whisper. Marko turned. Karl was staring at the nearest soldier.

"It scares me how I can't feel anything. That man is someone's brother or husband, but all I see is an enemy. I might as well be lying dead on this lake myself."

"Don't say that," Marko said. "You'll feel different when the war is over."

"How can you be so sure?"

"A soldier can't think or feel too much if he wants to survive. But my mother always said that time is a great healer. And—" Marko saw something move to his right.

"What is it?" Karl asked.

Just then a voice called, "Hey, it's Gimpy and his buddy." Juho and Seppo were skiing toward them.

Marko stared at their overstuffed packs. He knew who'd been stripping medals from the soldiers.

"What are you lookin' at?" Seppo said. "We got a right to collect souvenirs."

Juho nodded. "Payback time."

"You ladies lost?" Seppo said.

"We're supposed to find a squad out here," Karl said.

"We ain't seen nobody but dead Russkies." Seppo spat into the snow.

"So—" Marko began.

"So you girls will just have to follow your noses. But you'd better hurry, because this little tiff with the Russkies will be over real soon." Juho laughed as they skied away.

When the boys reached the far end of the lake, Marko noticed smoke rising from behind a hill. "Must be the squad."

The boys skied over a low ridge and into a clearing, surprised to find a smoldering fire pit but no men.

Marko shook his head. "Juho and Seppo must have cooked their coffee here."

"Idiots!" Karl said. "They didn't even put it out."

Marko slipped off his skis and knelt to rake some snow over the coals. "Those two have got to be the biggest—"

Marko was interrupted by the pop of an artillery gun. He held his breath until the shell exploded back at camp.

"I was afraid they were zeroing in on this," Karl said.

"Let's get clear," Marko said as a red squirrel chattered in the tree above their heads and steam rose from the fire pit.

But before Marko could plant his poles and ski away, he heard another pop followed by a high-pitched whizzing. "Cover!"

He and Karl dove into the snow. Marko's mind flashed back to the lieutenant announcing that the war was over. *Don't let us die! Not here. Not now.*

The force of the blast flung Marko sideways and knocked him to the ground. His left ski released, but his right strap held, twisting his leg under him.

Clods of dirt and bits of bark rattled down as a second and third shell screamed in.

CHAPTER 30

THE DRAG

Marko woke up lying facedown in the snow. His ears buzzed from the blast concussion, and he was wet and cold. "Karl!" he called, lifting his head.

No one answered. Marko sat up. Soot and dirt covered the snow. The fire was out.

"Marko . . . I'm hit."

Marko stood up and stretched the leg that he'd twisted as he fell; then he limped over to Karl.

"My leg hurts bad." The right side of Karl's face was black with soot.

Marko's heart stopped. A pink circle was spreading into the snow under Karl's right leg. "I'll take a look," Marko said.

Karl groaned as Marko slid his pants leg up. Shrapnel

had sliced open the back of Karl's leg, and his long underwear was soaked with blood. Marko felt faint.

"How is it?" Karl asked.

"Just a scratch," Marko lied. His mind raced. *What can I do?* "I'll get Seppo and Juho." He couldn't lose a second friend!

Marko jumped up. *Seppo and Juho can't be too far—* He stopped when he saw the shadows. He'd been knocked out for a long while. That was why his pants were so wet. Seppo and Juho were probably at camp by now. He couldn't believe they hadn't come back to see if he and Karl were all right.

He would have to help Karl himself. First he needed to stop the bleeding. He skied to the nearest Russian corpse. Trying not to look at the man's face, he pulled out his knife and cut wide strips of coarse wool from the coat.

He hurried back to Karl. "Here we go," Marko panted as he knelt. He hoped that Karl couldn't feel his hands shake as he wrapped a clean handkerchief over the wound. Then he picked up a strip of the heavy cloth.

"It burns . . . Marko . . ." Karl's voice sounded faint.

"This should help," Marko said, tying the wool around his leg. "Now we'll get you to camp."

Marko could ski back for help, or he could drag Karl with him. The snow was firm, but what could he use for a litter?

"Is my leg bad?"

"The medics will fix it up," Marko said.

The truth was that with such major blood loss Karl needed to get to a hospital fast.

Marko had lost Johan on the first day of the war—he was not going to let Karl die on the last day. If Marko cut across the lake and reached the road, he could flag down one of the sleighs heading to town. "I'll rig up some sort of litter."

"You could never carry me," Karl said. "Just get help."

Karl's eyes were closed, and he sounded as if he was ready to fall asleep. If Marko left him alone, he might go into shock and never wake up. "I'll find something!" Marko looked back at the Russian equipment strewn over the ice. "You stay awake. You hear me? I'll be right back."

Marko rushed back to the fallen horses and sleigh. His Civil Guard instructors had told him to improvise. He remembered a wooden handle in a snowdrift. When he found the handle, a quick jerk freed a canvas stretcher. He knocked off the snow. It was made for two men to carry, but he would have to make it work.

He dragged it back to Karl. "You awake?" Marko's throat was raw, and his head still ached from the shell blast.

"Everything looks fuzzy."

"Keep your eyes open!" Marko spied a young aspen. "I'm going to cut some sticks." He took out his knife and hacked off two forked branches.

"Now"—Marko pulled a rope out of his pack and cut off a short piece—"I'll lash these together with the forks facing out."

"You're crazy if you think that will work," Karl said.

"Just watch." Marko wedged the forks between the stretcher poles. "Tight as a drum." He thumped the canvas.

"Not . . . very musical." Karl tried to smile.

Marko lashed the forked ends in place. "Ready for a ride?"

"Just leave me."

"And not use this rig?" Marko picked up the front poles and dragged the stretcher a few meters to test it.

Then he looked at Karl's wound. Blood had soaked through the bandage. If it bled much more, Marko might have to use his rope to tie on a tourniquet. Civil Guard class had taught him to use a tourniquet only in a dire emergency, because cutting off the circulation could cause damage. "But if you ever have to choose," the instructor said, "don't hesitate to sacrifice a limb to save a life." Marko hoped he could control Karl's bleeding without risking the loss of his leg.

In class when they'd practiced putting on a tourniquet, Johan said, "If the Russians shoot you, let's hope they hit your bad leg." It had been easy to laugh on that summer day, so far from battlefields and real bandages.

Marko laid the stretcher beside Karl. "We'll slide you on. Then you lie back and take it easy. Lift your hips." Marko helped Karl. "Now one leg at a time."

Karl gritted his teeth as he moved his good leg on his own, but when Marko lifted his wounded leg, Karl shrieked.

"Sorry!" Marko said.

"What about . . . our skis?"

"I wish I could pull this and ski, but I'll have to walk." Marko stuck both pairs in a snowbank. "They'll be safe here."

Marko bent down and lifted the front of the stretcher. "You need to eat more potatoes."

"You won't say that a kilometer from now," Karl said.

Marko's first step made the stretcher bounce. "Watch the bumps," Karl groaned.

The rear poles of the stretcher slid easily across the frozen snow, and once Marko was moving, Karl felt even lighter. Marko set off across the lake.

As they passed the dead horses and the sleigh, he tried to distract Karl. "Silly of you to get wounded in the last minutes of the war."

"Just wanted . . . to give you something to complain about."

"The exercise will do me good," Marko said. "Did I ever tell you about the time Paavo Nurmi walked ten kilometers to Paris right after he won two gold medals?"

As Marko told the Paavo Nurmi stories, the leg that he'd twisted began to ache.

Marko passed a frozen tank with icicles dripping from its cannon barrel, and the body of a capless Russian soldier, sitting in the snow with his legs crossed. The man had one hand under his bearded chin and looked like he was dreaming. A snowdrift covered his back.

Marko looked at Karl. His face was ashen and his eyes half closed. "My mother taught me a trick that really helps block the pain," Marko said. "She had me think of a place that was calm and peaceful. How about your farm?"

"Not the farm," Karl said. "All I can see are the black eyes of that soldier and me reaching for the shovel."

"My special place is a bay where my friend Johan and I used to go swimming," Marko said. "Just offshore there's an island with a rock ledge that's perfect for sunbathing."

"Just let me rest."

"No! Stay awake! If I'm going to all the trouble to drag you across this lake, the least you can do is listen to my stories." Karl smiled weakly. Marko knew that if Karl passed out, he might never wake up again.

"The island has a deep drop-off on one end that's perfect for diving. One day Johan and I swam right up to a loon. . . ."

Trying not to pant, Marko talked as he dragged the stretcher over the place where the lake had been mined. A faint smell of gasoline was the only hint of the battle. Ice had sealed the scar where the tanks had disappeared.

By the time Marko reached the far shore, he'd told Karl the story of his day swimming with Johan, and how his polio began. He set the stretcher down to catch his breath. "That day was the last time I ever walked without this." He rapped his brace. His body ached as though he was getting polio all over again.

"Are we there yet?" Karl asked.

"You sound like my little sister," Marko said. "We

made it across the lake." The day was so warm that Marko was sweating, but Karl's lips looked blue. "Are you cold?"

"A little." Karl's voice trembled.

Marko took off his coat and tucked it around Karl's shoulders. Marko smiled. "That's a pretty good imitation."

"Of what?"

"You're making a face just like Kekko does."

"My face is twisted . . . 'cause I hurt," Karl said.

"I thought you were trying to make me laugh," Marko said. He picked up the stretcher and started pulling again.

"I know how much you're hurting. Leave me here."

"I won't leave you no matter what," Marko said.

"What are you . . . most afraid of, Marko?"

"That you're never going to stop asking me questions." The bank ahead was steeper than he remembered.

"Seriously," Karl said.

"When it comes right down to it"—Marko started up the bank—"I'm most afraid . . . I'll never be normal. That people won't . . . really see who I am because of my leg. A girl wouldn't ever like me. And who knows if I'll ever be strong enough to do a man's work?"

"Someone will like you."

"Easy for you to say," Marko said as he picked his way between the rocks and tall pines.

"I know it," Karl said.

"What's your biggest fear?" Marko asked.

"Going back . . . home . . . alone." Karl's voice trembled. "I shake every time I think about walking into my house again."

"You don't have to worry about going anywhere alone. We're in this together."

CHAPTER 31

THE CLIMB

Marko plodded up the hill, trying not to jostle Karl. He saw that Karl had closed his eyes again. "If you don't stay awake, I'll try to guess your name."

"Give up . . . on that," Karl said.

"The war's over," Marko said. "No reason to keep it a secret."

"Maybe I won't ever tell you."

Marko's heart pounded, and sweat poured down his forehead. At the top of the hill, he set the stretcher down. He took off his cap and stuffed it into his back pocket. "I'm sweating like I've been at our forge all day."

Karl was pale, and his eyes were closed.

"Hey!" Marko said. "You said my driving was too rough for you to sleep." He gave Karl tea from his canteen. Karl closed his eyes again.

"At least tell me the first letter of your name." 203

"It hurts bad, Marko."

"Picture something peaceful, like that day Johan and I were swimming with the loon." Marko rubbed the back of his calf. Then he picked up the stretcher.

"How can I . . . relax but not sleep?" Karl's tongue sounded thick.

"Tell me a story," Marko said.

"Too tired."

"Come on, now," Marko said. "Think back to something that happened before the war."

"I do remember a time . . . last November. It was late in the day. Father and I had dropped off some sacks of rye at the flour mill." Karl's voice sounded far away. "When we stepped outside and climbed into the wagon . . . the sky was totally black, like a ghost city. I was scared until I remembered the blackout."

Karl took a shallow breath. "On the way home snow started falling. . . . A car came toward us . . . and snow-flakes swirled in the slits of the headlights. Then it was dark."

"Virtalinna was the same," Marko said. "Like everyone had packed up and gone away."

"Now everyone will have to go," Karl said.

"Let's not think about that," Marko said as he passed the place where the Finnish gunners had fired their cannons. "Remember those big guns?"

"My head aches just thinking about it," Karl said. "If only I could sleep a little."

"No sleeping!"

In a few minutes Marko reached a clearing. "I know

this place. Last fall Johan and I ran an orienteering course through here."

"Let's hope I don't end up like Johan," Karl sighed.

"Never! Don't talk that way." The thought of Karl dying was too much for Marko. "Just one little bog ahead, then the road."

Karl was silent.

"Talk to me, Karl." Marko looked over his shoulder and saw that Karl's eyes were shut. "If you don't talk, I'll have to sing a funny song, 'My Pretty Darling.' 'My darling is so very pretty. With her skinny bones and her knotted hair, with her squinty eyes and her yard-wide mouth, she makes the horses—' " He turned. "Hey! Don't you like my song?"

Karl blinked. "What?"

Marko had to hurry. He trotted through the bog, dodging the frozen hummocks.

"Whoa!" Karl almost slid off the stretcher.

The stick had slipped off the rear handles. He knelt and tied it back in place. "Good as new." But Karl's bandage had darkened. "I think I'll wrap another turn around this," Marko said. "Have a drink while I fix it." He handed Karl the canteen.

"Am I bleeding a lot?" Karl asked. His hands shook as he took a swallow of tea.

"Just want to play it safe," Marko said.

Marko tied another layer around the wound. He hoped he hadn't made a mistake trying to get to the road. If Karl bled to death, he would never forgive himself. But if Marko tied on a tourniquet and Karl lost his leg, Marko would always wonder if he could have waited.

"How much farther?" Karl asked.

"There's a farm up ahead, and the road should be just beyond it." Marko hoped it wouldn't snow. Low clouds were moving in from the west, and the sky was darkening.

"Starts . . . with a *K*," Karl said.

"What's that?"

"My name."

"You're finally going to tell me?"

"Three . . . guesses."

"*K* . . ." Marko thought. "It must be Kristiina."

"Not even close."

"Okay." Marko pulled the stretcher as fast as he could. "Katri?"

"Nah."

"I've got it—Katariina."

Karl didn't answer. Marko turned. Karl's eyes were closed, and he looked totally white.

At that same moment Marko heard a sleigh. "Be right back!"

Marko ran as fast as he could. At the edge of the field he hurdled a fence and somersaulted into the snow. But he scrambled back up.

He reached the edge of the road just as the horses clattered past. "Stop!"

The teamster didn't hear. Marko picked up a stick and threw it. It hit the teamster in the shoulder. The man whirled and aimed a rifle.

"Don't shoot!" Marko ducked and waited for the shot. *I'll be dead and Karl will be left in the woods to bleed to death.*

"Is that you, Koski?"

Marko jumped up and ran to the sleigh.

"What in blazes are you doing out here? Those last shellings made me so jumpy I was ready to shoot—"

"Karl's hurt bad. We need to get to the hospital."

CHAPTER 32

THE HOSPITAL ROOM

Marko opened his eyes and squinted in the harsh white light. It took him a moment to realize he was staring at the ceiling of his old classroom. Why was it so quiet? Then he saw he was wearing his soot-covered uniform and lying on top of a hospital bed. He remembered the doctor working on Karl's leg. Mother had talked Marko into lying down to rest by promising to wake him when the doctor was done. *Where is Mother? And Karl?*

Marko stepped into the hall, limping badly. Mother was just leaving the next room.

"Marko!" She turned and gave him a hug. "Look at you." She held him by the shoulders.

"How's Karl?" Marko asked.

"Don't worry. Karl is right in here and doing well.

But you do know"—Mother looked at him with worried eyes—"that Karl—"

"Is a girl." Marko nodded.

He stepped through the doorway. Karl was propped up on two pillows and wearing a white hospital gown. Her blue eyes were huge. Her blond hair had been washed, and it shone in the sunlight. "Good morning, K—" Marko stopped.

"It's Kaari," she said.

"I should have guessed."

"Are you mad at me?" Kaari asked.

"Why? After what we've lived through, we'll always be friends. It's like we're—"

"Blood brothers?"

"Yes, brothers. Baptized in the blood of battle." Marko smiled.

"You're not angry I made you keep my secret for so long?"

"It's not like I had to lie to anyone."

"That's true," Kaari laughed. As Marko listened to her musical laughter, he couldn't believe that he hadn't noticed she was a girl right off.

"Are you sure you can be friends with a girl?" Kaari asked.

"Friends stick by each other no matter what. How's your leg?"

"I should be asking you the same question," Kaari said.

"I'm used to it," Marko said. "How many stitches did you get?"

"Seventeen. And you told me it was only a scratch."

"Now you know why I didn't want you to go to sleep."

Mother nodded. "She was close to shock."

"You saved my life, Marko," Kaari said.

"You would have done the same for me."

That evening as Mother and Marko walked home from the hospital she shared the news from Sweden. "Grandmother's last letter said that Nina is getting along fine with her cousins, and she's even learning how to crochet."

"But she hated needlework," Marko said.

"Nina's also been helping an aid committee sew clothing for our troops. And Grandma says little Jari is babbling in Swedish—she's afraid that he may forget his Finnish."

Once inside the house, Mother handed him a letter. "Arrived yesterday. Father was finally able to tell where he'd been stationed."

"Was he in Suomussalmi?"

"How did you guess?"

"I knew he was in the north, and I heard about a big Red Army offensive in that sector." Marko picked up the letter.

"He was in the battle on the Raate road," Mother said.

Not the Raate road. "Is he all right?" If the Russians had lost a whole division, as Kerola said, how many Finns had been hurt or killed?

"Only frostbite on two toes. He's at a military hospital in Joensuu."

When Marko finished the letter he smiled. "Father says that losing a couple of toes won't hurt his black-smithing."

"We'll all be together again very soon." Mother looked out the window toward the field and the lake beyond. "If only we didn't have to leave this behind."

"It's not right that we go to bed having a home and wake up to find that politicians drew a line on a map and took it all away."

"That's why wars never stop," Mother said. "It's the greed of rich men with pencils in their hands."

"And how could the Russians give our people only two weeks to move?" Marko said.

"We have a lifetime of things to pack." Mother looked at her kitchen.

"I'll help you as soon as I get back."

"You're not going to the front!"

"My duty is with my company."

"But what if the Russians—"

"The shooting has stopped, but the army has lots of work to do. Any equipment we leave behind will be lost."

"But—"

"The war is over, Mother. And Father and I survived. Moving will be easy after what we've lived through."

Later, when Marko went to bed and stretched out under his feather quilt, he expected to fall right to sleep.

But after a winter of snoring soldiers and bombard-ments, he couldn't stand the quiet. He turned over and stared at the dark ceiling. He finally pulled his bedding onto the wooden floor and slept.

Later, a voice rose. A soldier, singing softly and smil-ing, walked toward Marko. "I'm home," he said.

Then Marko saw that the soldier was clutching his guts in his hands. He screamed.

Mother ran in. "A bad dream?" She squeezed his hand.

Marko opened his eyes, but the image of the smiling soldier wouldn't go away. "I'm sorry." Marko's scalp prickled with fear.

"How you must have suffered!" Mother said.

"I'll be fine."

"Try to rest," Mother said. "Some of the boys in the hospital have nightmares at first. But they go away with time."

Marko nodded. But after she left he was afraid to close his eyes. He looked out the silver window at the stars. Despite the fresh sheets that smelled of a cool spring day, Marko knew it would be a long time before he could forget the stink of spent powder and death.

CHAPTER 33

THE REPORTER

When Marko arrived back at camp, Joki shouted to him. "You got here just in time to miss the work, messenger boy."

"What do you mean?"

Kekko said, "Can't you see we got everything packed?"

"Didn't have to load no bullets, though," Joki said. "We shot 'em all at the Russkies."

Marko looked at the sleighs. Everything but the sleeping tents had been loaded. Even the soup cannon had been wheeled out of the woods and was ready to be hitched to a team.

"At least you can help us break down the tents in the morning," Kekko said.

"So how'd it turn out with Karl?" Joki asked. "The
teamster said he got hit pretty hard."

"He's limping"—Marko thought of saying *she* but
didn't want to get into a long explanation—"but the
doctor says he's going to be fine."

"That's good to hear," Kekko said.

"The lieutenant put Juho and Seppo on report for
starting that fire," Joki said. "Them fools! Thinking the
Russkies won't shell a smoke plume is like counting on
a short fuse not to burn fast."

"But all of us have done dumb stuff," Kekko said.

"Like taking a sauna in broad daylight behind enemy lines?" It was the lieutenant, walking up the hill.

"We don't need to bring that up," Kekko said.

Marko woke up late the next morning. Sunlight filtered through the tent roof, but the men were still snoring. He heard strange voices outside and pulled on his
boots.

Juhola had just finished shaving over his helmet. He held his razor in his hand, and a towel hung
over his shoulder. A reporter and a photographer
dressed in civilian overcoats and hats were standing beside him.

"It's an American magazine that you write for?" The
lieutenant spoke in Finnish to a translator, who re-
peated the question to the reporter, who was writing in
a notebook.

"Yes."

"Tell me, please, how could your president have believed Stalin's lies?" Juhola set down his razor.

The reporter stopped writing. "With Hitler building up his army and all, he probably had too much on his mind."

"Your Congress talked of sending help." The lieutenant had remained calm through so many battles, but now he was angry. "Instead, they delivered seventy million dollars' worth of machine tools to Russia! We believed in America, even as your companies were selling ammunition to the Russians and shipping Liberty engines to their tank factories. Liberty!" He looked to the east. "In the end we stood alone.

"Now we have lost Karelia. Twenty-five thousand of our brave soldiers are dead. More than four hundred thousand Finnish people are homeless."

"I only want a story," the reporter said.

"A story?" The lieutenant's voice was cold. "Nice that you have come to do your reporting now that the bullets have stopped. If you want to tell a story, it is there in that valley"—he pointed down the hill—"written in the trenches with the blood of good men."

The soldiers were quiet when the time came to hitch up the sleighs and leave camp. The minute Joseph saw Marko he nickered, but his ears drooped when he noticed that Karl wasn't with him. "Sorry, boy," Marko said as he stroked Joseph and Cheslav.

Before Company Three pulled out, Marko walked to

the rim of the hill and looked down on Savolahti one last time. The air smelled like spring. Clear droplets of snowmelt hung from the needles of the pines.

Below, Marko saw the red chimney of the pottery factory and the blackened timbers of Grandma's barn. Grandma had been certain her farm would be rebuilt. But now there would be no more Christmas sleigh rides to Savolahti. No more saunas during haying time. No more mushroom picking on the aspen hillsides.

The men were silent during the long march to Virtalinna. Marko was surprised at how weak the battle-hardened soldiers looked. Under the bright sun their skin was ghostly white and their eyes bloodshot. Many of them coughed badly, and they had stained teeth and bleeding gums. Those who had washed and shaved looked the worst, because their sunken cheeks and eye sockets stood out. Some of the fellows rested a hand on the wagon as they walked or used a ski pole as a walking stick. For once Marko's limp fit right in.

The horses were all bones, too, and looked ready to topple over. "Poor nags," Kekko said. "They sure never done nothing to deserve this."

When the company stopped for a cold lunch, Joki looked up and down the road and said, "I can't get it into my head . . . this is gonna be Russian territory two weeks from now."

"Me neither." Kekko nodded. "What kind of a world is it that we beat back the Russkies at every turn, and our government goes and signs away a big chunk of territory? Think of all the boys we sent home shot to pieces."

"And all that got fitted for wooden overcoats," Hoot said.

"It's like the blood and guts was spilled for nothing," Joki said.

Marko nodded. "Everything I've ever known is gone. Grandma's farm. Virtalinna. All the land in between. Gone."

"I don't want you boys ever to think that way." It was the lieutenant, riding Kahvi. "Yes, the cost was dear. But by holding that line we guaranteed Finland her freedom. Politics may have shortchanged us in the near term, but in our hearts we know we won. Besides, a great man once said, 'There never was a good war, or a bad peace.'"

"And we taught the Russkies a lesson they won't never forget," Joki said.

"We showed 'em what we're made of," Kekko said. "We showed the world!"

"Knowing what you men are made of scares me a whole lot more than the Russians ever did." Juhola smiled as he rode on ahead.

CHAPTER 34

FLAGS UNFURLED

Marko found Mother in the hospital.

"Marko! At last!" She hugged him tightly. "I was so afraid there'd be one more attack."

"How's Kaari?" Marko asked.

"See for yourself!"

When Marko stepped into the room, Kaari was leaning on crutches and looking out the first-floor window at Kronholm Castle.

"Aren't you supposed to be resting?"

"Marko!" She hobbled over to give him a hug.

"Careful." Marko could feel her trembling from the effort of walking.

"I'll be ready to race you by summer," she said, sitting back on the edge of the bed.

"Pick a long course so I can win."

"Distance always was your specialty," Kaari said.

"So . . . what will you do now?" Marko sat down beside her. "Where will you go?"

"Your mother and I were just talking about that."

"I'm sure she wasn't shy about giving advice."

Kaari smiled. "According to the paper, the border near my village won't change."

"So you haven't lost your home!"

Kaari nodded. "But if I wanted to go back, I couldn't run the farm on my own even after I got better."

"You'll need someone to look out for you at first," Marko said.

"That's where your mother comes in. I had an idea and asked her to think about it. She said she'd talk it over with you."

"What sort of idea?"

"Since you've lost your home, I told her that you'd all be welcome to move to my farm. I don't have any relatives to help me, and I know you'd love my village." Kaari talked faster as she got more excited. "There's a blacksmith shop up the road from my house that would be perfect for your father. And the neighbors have children the same age as Jari and Nina. Why, even your grandmother would be wel—"

"Let's not get too far ahead of ourselves. Sounds like you and Mother have been doing a lot of planning."

"She says I need time to heal and put my life back together. And now that I'm an orphan, it would be perfect if . . . if a family would adopt me. And if that family

had a strong young man who was good at chopping
wood and digging holes—"

"And skiing fast?"

"That would be even better," Kaari said.

"We're already brothers," Marko said, grinning at
Kaari. "You might as well be my sister, too!"

Marko looked down at the marks on the wooden
floor that showed where the school desks had stood last
fall. "This is too much to take in all at once. Here I am in
my old school, trying to get used to the idea that I've lost
my home, and you and Mother have my whole family
moving to a new town."

"I told you that I could never go back to my farm
alone . . . after what happened."

"I know." Marko squeezed Kaari's hand. "And I
was afraid my family would have to move to Sweden. A
new life on a new farm sounds better than becoming
refugees."

"And we need to show the Russians—"

"That we can build our country back up." Marko
nodded.

Kaari looked through the window at Kronholm
Castle. "A Lotta told me those flags will be lowered for
the last time this afternoon. I can't believe Johan lived in
such a beautiful castle!"

"Yes, that was his home." Marko stared as the flags
of Finland and Sweden unfurled in the breeze.

"It must be close to the time," Kaari said.

Marko stepped over and opened the window partway. The air smelled of melting snow and buds soon to

open. The shadows of the buildings and the trees extended out over the empty marketplace.

Suddenly a trumpet began to play the Finnish national anthem in the courtyard of the castle. "There they go," Kaari whispered, walking to Marko's side as the flags were slowly lowered. Marko's eyes filled with tears.

"I loved visiting the castle when I was little," he said. "The stone walls looked like they'd stand forever. And I could see those flags from everywhere in town. They gave me a feeling that . . . all was well." He shook his head. "It's hard to believe they'll never be going up again."

"You may have lost your town," Kaari told Marko, touching his shoulder, "but you helped save our country."

"That's what the lieutenant said."

"Finland proved she could stand alone against the world," Kaari said.

"Like us," Marko said.

"Like us."

"Hey, messenger boy." Marko was shocked to see Kekko and Joki walk through the doorway. Both men wore civilian clothes, though Kekko still had on his helmet with its broken chin strap. "Your momma said we'd find you here."

At the same time a horse nickered outside the window.

"Joseph!" Marko said as the big bay pushed his nose through the window and nuzzled Kaari's hand. Cheslav stood right beside Joseph.

"The army was going to auction them horses off as surplus property, but the lieutenant figured they'd be better off with you and Karl." Kekko looked around the room. "Where is Karl?"

Before Marko could answer, Kekko went on. "But the real reason we came over here was to tell you about the fireworks. We're planning a little show."

"The war is over," Marko said.

"Not quite," Joki said. "Kekko and I decided we don't want Russian visitors bothering us once we move across the river."

"You're not going to blow up the bridge!" Marko said.

"We tried to run the idea past the lieutenant, but he stopped us and said, 'Don't tell me any more, boys. You're on leave now, and it's not my place to give you orders.' "

"So we set up some barricades," Kekko said. "Hoot's down there now, making sure the folks keep clear."

Marko looked at the road below the castle. A crowd of people had gathered to watch the explosion. "But how will we get across the river?" Marko asked.

"The ice is plenty solid," Kekko said. "But by the time the Russkies get here, they'll have to swim."

"Or take up boat-building," Joki said.

"Hoot must be about ready," Kekko said

Joki pulled out his watch. "Any second now."

Kekko suddenly noticed Kaari. "Who's the girl?"

"This is Karl!" Marko said.

"What?" Kekko stared at Kaari.

"Don't you recognize your fellow soldier?" Kaari asked.

"That's his voice!" Joki said.

Kaari and Marko burst out laughing.

"Yes, I had a secret, didn't I?" she said.

Kekko's mouth dropped open. "But how—"

At that same instant the first charge exploded.

Joki looked out the window. "There she blows!"

Marko turned. Smoke and flames flashed out from under the bridge as the rest of the dynamite exploded. Chunks of stone and mortar flew in all directions; the shock wave that followed rattled the hospital windows.

Time froze as the dust billowed upward and the stone pilings crumbled apart in slow motion. The bridge deck sagged, suspended by nothing for an instant before it hit the ice with a shuddering crash that shot water high into the air.

Marko smiled as bits of debris fell on the street and the marketplace, pattering on the cobblestones like a gentle rain. In the sunset above the shattered pilings the dust cloud glowed red, while the people standing in the shadows of the castle raised their arms and cheered.

AFTERWORD

The Finns who are a people of the North and very athletic, can ski almost before they can walk. Our army encountered very mobile ski troops armed with automatic high velocity rifles. We tried to put our own troops on skis, too, but it wasn't easy for ordinary, untrained Red Army soldiers to fight on skis. We started intensively to recruit professional sportsmen. There aren't many around. We had to bring them from Moscow and the Ukraine as well as Leningrad. We gave them a splendid send off. Poor fellows, they were ripped to shreds. I don't know how many came back alive.

> —Nikita Khrushchev, premier of the Soviet Union 1958–1964 (from his 1970 autobiography, *Khrushchev Remembers*)

When President Kyösti Kallio signed the Moscow peace agreement on March 13, 1940, ending the Winter War, he said, "Let the hand wither that signs this monstrous treaty!"

Shortly afterward, his right arm became paralyzed. His health worsened until the following November, when he collapsed and died of a massive stroke.

The sad end of President Kallio's life mirrored the national mourning that Finland experienced following the Winter War. Though Russia had been the aggressor, the terms imposed by the treaty were harsh. Finland surrendered thirty-five thousand square kilometers of land, including Karelia, a region rich in natural resources; Petsamo, Finland's outlet to the Barents Sea; and Porkkala, a peninsula very close to Helsinki that would be the site of a Russian military base. Four hundred thirty thousand Karelians, or 12 percent of Finland's population, were given a week to vacate their homes.

Finland's distrust of Russia dates back to 1809, the year Czar Alexander I took control of Finland and established a grand duchy. Relations worsened in 1898, when Nikolai Bobrikov became governor of Finland and began to exert total control. Russian became the official language of Finland, the Finnish parliament was disbanded, and Finnish men were drafted to fight in the czar's army.

On December 6, 1917, Finland declared its independence from Russia. The following month a civil war

broke out between Red and White forces within
Finland. Despite Russia's support of the Red side, after a winter of fierce fighting the White Army prevailed under the leadership of Carl Gustaf Mannerheim. The Finnish people worked hard to rebuild their shattered country. They cut back on military spending and put all their effort into establishing peace and prosperity.

However, in 1939, just as conditions were beginning to improve in Finland, Russia's dictator, Joseph Stalin, threatened to take territory from Finland's eastern border, citing "security reasons." President Kallio tried to negotiate a compromise, but Stalin chose to invade instead.

For 105 days, through one of the coldest winters in history, Finland fought to keep the Red Army at bay. Though overmatched in troop numbers by four-to-one odds and in tanks by a hundred to one, the Finns put on white camouflage suits and fought a guerilla war with such courage and skill that their techniques are still studied by military academies throughout the world.

In the end, Finnish casualties totaled 25,000, the 1940 equivalent of the United States' losing 2.5 million people. Approximately 50,000 Finns were wounded, and of the 84,000 Lotta Svärd volunteers, 64 women were killed. The total number of Russian dead and wounded is impossible to verify, but it exceeded 500,000.

During the course of the war, Finland got sympathy from the world but little material aid. The shining exceptions were Sweden, which contributed a fighter plane wing along with nine thousand soldiers (accompanied by one thousand Norwegians), and Denmark, which sent a corps of trained pilots. Small groups of volunteer soldiers arrived from other countries, but they were too disorganized to be effective.

When Finland attempted to purchase armaments from other countries, the shipments were often delayed—Germany blocked a major fighter plane order from Italy—or they arrived too late to help. The main source of weapons and ammunition ended up being booty that Finland seized from the Russians early in the war.

A major aftereffect of the Winter War was its influence on Hitler. When Hitler saw the difficulty Stalin had in defeating a small country such as Finland, he mistakenly assumed that the Russians would be an easy target. However, Stalin learned from his mistakes, and he made major changes in his army, the most dramatic being the recall of experienced officers whom he'd discharged during the Winter War.

After the Winter War, Finland tried to gain back the land it had ceded to Russia. As World War II intensified and Estonia, Latvia, and Lithuania were annexed by Russia, Finland felt it would be next if it didn't launch an offensive. The Continuation War, as it's known in Finland, went well at first. Mannerheim's troops swept across Karelia and reoccupied the territory for two and a half years.

Unfortunately, when the Continuation War ended, Finland had to give up Karelia for good. And to make matters worse, the Allies allowed Stalin to impose on Finland $225 million in reparations. Many of the materials he demanded were engineering goods and machinery that Finland did not manufacture.

Unlike most countries, which avoided paying their war debts, Finland went to work, and in only eight years delivered eighty turbogenerators, seven hundred locomotives, fifty thousand motors and engines, and six hundred ships. This production put a strain on the Finnish economy and forced the people to lead a spartan life, but in the long run, it helped make Finland one of the most technologically advanced countries in the world.

WINTER WAR SOURCES FOR FURTHER STUDY

Documentary Film

Fire and Ice: The Winter War of Finland and Russia
Web site featuring film trailers and still shots:
www.mastersworkmedia.com/fireandice

Books

The Winter War: The Soviet Attack on Finland 1939–1940, by Eloise Engle, Lauri Paananen, and Eloise Paananen

A Frozen Hell: The Russo-Finnish Winter War of 1939–40, by William R. Trotter

Molotov Cocktail, the Russo-Finnish Winter War, 1939–1940: Finland's Pearl Harbor, by John O. Virtanen

Appeal That Was Never Made: The Allies, Scandinavia, and the Finnish Winter War, 1939–1940, by Jukka Nevakivi

The White Death: The Epic of the Soviet-Finnish Winter War, by Allen F. Chew

The Winter War, by Antti Tuuri
The classic adult Finnish war novel, translated by Richard Impola

Battles of the Winter War
www.winterwar.com/mainpage.htm

A day-by-day description of the Winter War,
including photographs
www.mil.fi/perustietoa/talvisota_eng/index.html

Winter War reenactors Web site
www.kevos4.com

The Winter War, an article by Robert Maddock Jr.
www.kaiku.com/winterwar.html

Winter War fighter planes
www.sci.fi/~fta/fintac-3.htm

ACKNOWLEDGMENTS

I'd like to extend special thanks to a number of people who were most generous in helping me with my research. Primary among them were Eero Juhola, a dedicated scholar and Winter War reenactor from Tuusula, Finland; Reima Rannikko, a retired teacher from Suomussalmi, Finland, who served in the Junior Civil Guard; Ovia Ylonen and Aune Nokkala, who provided me with a private translation of the authoritative work on the history of the Finnish Junior Civil Guard, *Poikasotilaista Sotilaspoikiin;* Suoma Joutsi, a former member of the Lotta Svärd; Matti Saarivirtta and Olavi Luhtanen, Winter War veterans; James Kuurti, editor of the *Finnish American Reporter;* Sirpa Haapala of the Finnish Polio Association; Leo Pelwa, a polio survivor;

Bobbie Kleffman and Allan Holmer, for helping out with horse questions; and the following Finnish cultural experts: Alpo Rissinen, Börje Vähämäki, Varpu Lindstrom, Ron Maki, Clyde Koskela, Bob Maki, Annikka Ojala, Carl Pellonpaa, Marshall Kregel, Anja Bottila, Sinikka Garcia, Rainer Makirinne, and Pentti Mahonen.

And as always, my gratitude goes to my editor, Wendy Lamb, who never fails to surprise me with her insights; to my agent, Barbara Markowitz, who is both an advocate and friend; to my wife, Barbara, who always gives me the soundest advice; and to my family, Jessica, Darren, Reid, and Autumn, for their continued understanding and support.

ABOUT THE AUTHOR

William Durbin was born in Minneapolis and lives on Lake Vermilion at the edge of the Boundary Waters Canoe Area Wilderness in northeastern Minnesota. He formerly taught English at a small rural high school and composition at a community college and has supervised writing research projects for the National Council of Teachers of English, the Bingham Trust for Charity, and Middlebury College. His wife, Barbara, is also a teacher, and they have two grown children. William Durbin has published biographies of Tiger Woods and Arnold Palmer, as well as several books for young readers, among them *The Broken Blade, Wintering, Song of Sampo Lake, Blackwater Ben,* and *El Lector. The Broken Blade* won the Great Lakes Book Award for Children's Books and the Minnesota Book Award for Young Adult Fiction. For more information, visit his Web site: williamdurbin.com.

Durbin, William,
1951-

The Winter War.